BRISTOL AT HOME LIBRARY SERVICE
Tel: 0117 903 8531   BM

He pulled her into his arms and brought his mouth down hard onto her own.

She was left gasping when equally abruptly he drew back, while still continuing to hold her.

'And that's something else I've been wanting to do all day,' he said. 'From the moment I saw you in that dress and that straw hat you were wearing I've wanted to do that.'

'You shouldn't...' she said, shaking her head. 'You mustn't, Omar...'

'Now, tell me you also haven't wanted that to happen?' He lowered his head slightly in order to look into her face. 'Sandie...?' he persisted when she didn't answer. 'No? Well, I'll tell you what I think. I think you wanted me to do that every bit as much as I wanted to. I've been aware of you all day, just as I know you have been aware of me. When we danced you melted in my arms...just like this...' Almost roughly he tightened his grip again and, pulling her closer, he once more covered her mouth with his own.

Laura MacDonald was born and bred in the Isle of Wight, where she still lives with her husband. The Island is a place of great natural beauty and forms the backdrop for many of Laura's books. She has been writing fiction since she was a child. Her first book was published in the 1980s and she has been writing full-time since 1991, during which time she has produced over forty books for both adults and children. When she isn't writing her hobbies include painting, reading and researching family history.

Recent titles by the same author:

A VERY SPECIAL SURGEON*
MEDITERRANEAN RESCUE
UNDER SPECIAL CARE*

Eleanor James Memorial Hospital

THE DOCTOR'S SPECIAL CHARM

BY
LAURA MacDONALD

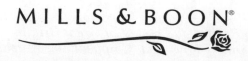

MILLS & BOON®

*First published in Great Britain 2004
Large Print edition 2005
Harlequin Mills & Boon Limited,
Eton House, 18-24 Paradise Road,
Richmond, Surrey TW9 1SR*

© Laura MacDonald 2004

ISBN 0 263 18445 5

*Set in Times Roman 16½ on 18¼ pt.
17-0105-51729*

*Printed and bound in Great Britain
by Antony Rowe Ltd, Chippenham, Wiltshire*

CHAPTER ONE

SANDIE was late, she knew it, in spite of the fact that she had got up half an hour early—and this her first day back after six months away on a neonatal course. When she had finally arrived on Paediatrics, after battling with the traffic and at first not being able to find a parking space in the car park of the Eleanor James Memorial Hospital, it was to be told by a staff nurse whom she didn't recognise that she was expected in a staff meeting in the hospital library. It was usual procedure for a department's registrar to preside over these meetings so at least that meant a familiar face in Matt Forrester. Sandie liked Matt. They had worked closely together many times during her time on the special care baby unit where his wife, Louise, was sister in charge.

But when at last she pushed open the library door with the intention of slipping unobtrusively into a chair in the back row, it was to find that there was no sign of Matt and a stranger was presiding over the meeting. Matt would, no doubt, have ignored the fact that she was late, letting her take her place without drawing attention to the fact. This man obviously had other ideas for he stopped speaking in mid-sentence and waited, apparently for her to take her place. The only vacant chair was halfway along the next to back row, and instead of causing the least possible disturbance Sandie found to her embarrassment that heads were turning and eyes were upon her as she stumbled over shoes and bags.

At last she reached the chair. 'Dr Rawlings, I presume?' said the man before she could even sit down, and a titter ran round the room.

'Yes...' Sandie nodded and gulped.

'I'm so pleased you could spare us the time.'

She felt her cheeks flame at his sarcasm. It was only later, when she knew him better, that she would understand that it wasn't sarcasm—that every word he said was genuine.

'I'm sorry,' she mumbled as she sank into her seat. 'The traffic was horrendous.'

'Well, you're here now,' he said, 'and you haven't missed too much. If you see my sec-

retary afterwards, she will give you a printout of what you have missed.'

'Thank you,' she said, sinking further down into her seat before taking her notebook and pen out of her bag. Where was Matt, for goodness' sake, and who on earth was this man who seemed to have everyone hanging on his every word?

Once attention was finally shifted away from herself she glanced unobtrusively round the room. To her relief she discovered that Penny Wiseman, sister on Paediatrics, was there, together with Staff Nurse Emma Hollingsworth, who shot her a delighted grin. Seated beside them was Louise Forrester, but of her husband Matt there was no sign whatsoever. She began to make notes, somehow automatically taking down what the speaker was saying without really taking it in. Between sentences she found herself studying the man at the front of the room, without any further enlightenment as to who he was. He was of mixed origin, neither black nor white. Neither was he Asian, as were many of the doctors at Ellie's, for while his skin was caramel-coloured his black hair was not straight but closely covered his head in tiny, tight curls. His features were essentially European, but it was his almost regal bearing, the proud tilt of his head and his liquid dark eyes that attracted and held Sandie's attention.

When the meeting at last drew to a close he thanked everyone for attending then, amidst a scraping of chairs, Sandie found herself surrounded.

'Sandie—welcome back!' This was from Emma Hollingsworth.

'Good to have you back!' Penny kissed her on the cheek.

'We've missed you,' said Louise, then, glancing at her watch, she added, 'I must fly now, but we must catch up later.'

'Yes,' said Sandie, slightly overwhelmed by everyone's enthusiasm, 'we must. It's so good to see you all again.' Caught up in the general exodus, she paused for a moment and glanced back at the man who had conducted the meeting. Briefly his gaze met hers and just for one moment she thought he was about to come across and introduce himself, but his attention was distracted by secretary Amanda Cromer, who hadn't been at the meeting but who now strode purposefully into the room, obviously with the express intention of catching the man in question. He half raised one hand in Sandie's direction, then she turned away and allowed herself to be swept along with the others out of the library.

As Sandie began to make her way through the hospital corridors to the paediatric department, Emma hurried to catch up with her. 'It's really good to see you again, Sandie,' she said. 'The place quite simply hasn't been the same without you.'

'Well, it's good to be back,' Sandie replied. 'This is where I belong and no matter how good the conditions are on a course and how nice the people, you know it's only temporary and that there's no point in putting down any roots.' She paused and threw Emma a sidelong glance. 'I see there have been a few changes here whilst I've been away.'

'You could say that.' Emma nodded.

'So who was the guy back there?' Sandie jerked one thumb over her shoulder.

'The guy...?' Emma frowned then her face cleared. 'Oh,' she said, 'of course, you don't know, I was forgetting, what with it happening just after you had gone. He's the new paediatric registrar—rather dreamy, don't you think? His name's Omar—Omar Nahum.'

'So where's Matt?' asked Sandie in bewilderment.

'Ah, yes, well, good question. Matt, believe it or not, got his promotion.'

'Really?' Sandie stopped and stared at Emma. 'But that's wonderful. He wasn't expecting it yet, was he?'

'No, but our eminent consultant Neil Richardson was forced to take early retirement—his wife had a heart attack or something, and he wanted to spend more time with her. Anyway, they gave the post to Matt.'

'And this Dr Nah— What did you say his name was?'

'Dr Nahum,' Emma replied with a little chuckle, 'but everyone calls him Omar or Dr Omar. He was senior house officer on Obstetrics at the time. Anyway, he applied and got the post of paediatric reg. He's nice, Sandie, you'll like him. Everyone does.'

'So what else have I missed?' asked Sandie faintly.

'Well, the other big piece of news around here has also come out of Obstetrics.'

'Go on,' said Sandie, standing back for Emma to precede her as they reached the double doors that led onto the children's ward.

'It's Sister Ryan—she and Tom Fielding are getting married!'

'Ah,' said Sandie. 'Now, that I did know.'

'Oh.' Emma sounded disappointed.

'Yes,' said Sandie, 'because I received an invitation to their wedding.'

Seconds later both she and Emma were drawn into the busy, all-enveloping world of Ellie's children's ward with its brightly coloured walls, nursery-rhyme characters, books, toys, cots, its staff with coloured aprons covering their uniforms and, of course, with the children themselves—some desperately ill, others recovering, some accompanied by anxious parents, others alone. It was noisy, too, with the chatter of children and the sound of 'The Music Man' coming from the ward's CD player. Two children were in the play area, one sitting at a low, round table building a tower with small interlocking plastic bricks, and the other in the Wendy house. This was a world

that Sandie was only too happy to inhabit, a
world she had chosen, and now, as she paused
for a moment and looked around her, she felt
once again how good it was to be back. Some
things might have changed over a few months
but there would always be small children need-
ing help—they might be different children but
the need was the same.

With a little sigh she made her way to
Penny's office in order to spend some time
familiarising herself with case histories before
the consultants' morning round. Penny was
sorting though the patients' folders but she
looked up as Sandie tapped on the door and
entered the room.

'Ah, Sandie,' she said, 'am I glad to have
you back. We've had a junior doctor, young
man called Jeremy, while you've been away.
Now, don't get me wrong, I'm sure he's a
lovely lad, just as I'm sure he'll be a very good
doctor one day, but at the moment let's say
he's still a bit damp behind the ears. There
were times when he drove me to distraction, I
can tell you. He's moved on to A and E apparently—I can only imagine he'll have to
buck up his ideas down there.'

'It'll probably be the making of him,' said Sandie with a laugh. 'Either that or it will finish him off completely. Talking of doctors, I had no idea we had a new reg.'

'Oh, yes,' said Penny, her expression softening. 'Now, Omar, well, he's different altogether.'

'I fear I got off to a bad start with him,' said Sandie ruefully. 'And I'd really made up my mind to make an effort to be early for once as well.'

'Sandie, the day you are actually early will, I'm sure, go down in the record books,' said Penny with a laugh.

'Yes, I know...' Sandie pulled a rueful face. 'But on my first day back, and with a new reg as well...' She shook her head.

'Don't worry about it,' said Penny. 'He won't. He's so nice—you'll see.'

'So Emma was saying,' said Sandie.

'Sometimes I think he's too nice for his own good,' said Penny. 'People take advantage of him.'

'Surely he can take care of himself.' Sandie picked up a folder and began looking through it.

'Well, yes, but you can imagine the stir he caused here with those looks. Some of the staff have almost been falling over each other to attract his attention.'

'And have they been successful?' asked Sandie, raising one eyebrow.

'Some have,' Penny said, 'but our Dr Omar doesn't seem too interested in long-term commitment. The latest one to catch his eye is Amanda Cromer, no less. It'll be interesting to see which way that goes. Amanda, as we know, is tenacious to say the least.'

'Quite,' Sandie agreed, recalling how the secretary had waylaid the registrar after the meeting at a time when she must have known he would be in a hurry to get to ward rounds. 'Where's he from?' she asked curiously.

Penny had returned to her paperwork but she looked up at Sandie's question. 'From?' she repeated, and when Sandie nodded, she said, 'Well, I suppose he's British.'

'Well, his origins, then?'

'I understand his mother is English and for the most part he was brought up and educated in this country, but his father, apparently, was from Somalia.'

So that accounted for his colouring and those eyes, thought Sandie. Then, in an attempt to put all thoughts of the new registrar out of her mind, she turned her attention back to Penny and the tasks ahead of her.

'I've just had a call from A and E,' said Penny. 'They have a young boy who has been involved in a road accident. He has multiple fractures—femur, clavicle and pelvis. Apparently Matt and the orthopaedic consultant have been down there to see him— he's coming here before going to Theatre.'

'Do we have any other details?' asked Sandie.

'Yes...' Penny checked the notes she'd made. 'His name is Sam Wallis and he's eight years old.'

'Is there anyone with him?'

'Yes, his parents. It appears he was hit by a car on his way to school.'

'I'll stay around while he's admitted if you like,' said Sandie.

'Thanks.' Penny nodded gratefully. 'It's a bit chaotic around here this morning—I'm one nurse down and the agency hasn't sent a temp yet.'

'Who else is in at the moment?' Sandie glanced through the glass partition that separated Penny's office from the main ward, then, not waiting for a reply, went on, 'Who are the two in the play area?'

Penny craned her neck to see. 'That's Lewis Winter playing with the bricks,' she said. 'He and his family moved to the area fairly recently. Lewis unfortunately has a neuroblastoma—he's having a course of chemotherapy at the moment. The little girl is Gemma Sanderson—she is undergoing tests for a gastric problem but we don't have any answers yet. We also have a girl with Crohn's disease, a boy with cystic fibrosis, another undergoing allergy assessment, a baby with breathing problems... Shall I go on?'

'No, I get the picture,' said Sandie. 'A pretty full house by the sounds of it.'

'You can say that again.' Penny turned as the door opened and a nurse popped her head around. 'What is it, Kim?' she asked.

'The little boy from A and E has just arrived,' said the girl. Catching sight of Sandie, she added, 'Hello, Dr Rawlings—nice to see you back.'

'Thanks, Kim, it's nice to be back,' said Sandie. As Penny moved to the door she said, 'I'll just take a look around then I'll join you.'

'I imagine I may need some help with the parents,' said Penny, 'but we'll get the little lad admitted first.'

As Penny bustled off onto the ward to receive her latest charge Sandie also left the office and strolled across to the table where the little boy was still building his blocks into a tower. 'Hello,' she said, crouching down beside him. He was about six years old and the check cap he wore, no doubt to cover the ravages of his chemotherapy, gave him a cheeky, waif-like appearance. 'I'm Sandie. What's your name?'

. 'Lewis,' he said. Looking up from his bricks, he studied Sandie, apparently taking in every detail, from her dark hair and green eyes to the white coat she wore open over her crisp white blouse and black trousers, his gaze finally coming to rest on the stethoscope protruding from the top pocket of her coat. 'I haven't seen you before,' he added at last.

'I've been away,' said Sandie.

'On holiday?' asked Lewis.

'No, not on holiday. I've been working but in another hospital.' She paused. 'How are you feeling this morning?'

'All right.' He shrugged. 'I was sick when I woke up, but I'm all right now.'

'Well, that's good.' Sandie glanced up as the little girl who had been playing in the Wendy house suddenly backed out and turned to face them, her hair dishevelled from the exertion, her face bright red and her eyes bright. 'Who's your friend?' she asked Lewis.

'She isn't my friend,' said Lewis, a note of scorn in his voice. 'That's Gemma—she's only a baby.'

'I'm not a baby!' Tears filled the little girl's eyes and Sandie reached out and took one small hand in hers. 'Hello, Gemma,' she said. 'I'm Sandie.'

'She's a doctor,' said Lewis.

'I want Dr Omar.' The tears overflowed and began trickling down the little girl's cheeks.

'I'm sure he'll be along to see you later,' said Sandie. 'Have you been giving the dolls their breakfast?' she asked, peering into the Wendy house where she could see a plastic tea set on a small table.

Gemma nodded and stuck one finger in her mouth.

'Do you think I could have a cup of tea?' Sandie added.

'It's not real tea,' said Lewis, as Gemma toddled back into the Wendy house.

'I know,' said Sandie softly. 'It's pretend tea, just like the tower you're building is a pretend skyscraper.' Lewis looked at his bricks and considered what she had said. 'Shall I help you?' she added.

'If you like,' he said, moving aside so that she could join him on the plastic bench.

So engrossed did she become in helping Lewis with his skyscraper and drinking the imaginary tea that Gemma brought her that it wasn't until she looked up to find a sea of faces looking down at her that she realised in dismay that the consultants had arrived for their morning round.

Matt was there, dear Matt, looking every inch the successful consultant paediatrician in his charcoal suit, together with his fellow paediatrician Suzanne Purcell. They were accompanied by the orthopaedic surgeon and the oncologist and, of course, the paediatric registrar,

Omar Nahum. For the second time that day Sandie found herself in the somewhat uncomfortable position of being the centre of attention. Predictably it was Matt who defused the situation and came to her rescue.

'Sandie,' he said. Stepping forward, he took her hands and drew her to her feet. That in itself would have been sufficient, but as he welcomed her back to his department he gave her a hug. 'It's good to see you again,' he said.

'Thank you, Dr Forrester,' she replied, mindful of his newly acquired status and the company they were in. 'I understand congratulations are in order.'

'Is anyone going to introduce me to this lovely lady?' Omar Nahum had stepped forward. 'I feel at a decided disadvantage because the rest of you all seem to know her and I do not.'

'Omar, I'm sorry.' It was Matt who responded. 'I'd forgotten. You came to us after Sandie left. Sandie, this is Dr Omar Nahum, who is now our registrar. Omar, this is Sandie Rawlings. Sandie was SHO here on the department before going off to Manchester to complete her neonatal course. I for one am delighted she is back—she has been sorely missed. Isn't that right, Sister Wiseman?'

'You can say that again,' said Penny dryly.

Sandie was aware that her hands had been taken again, both of them, grasped in a firm, cool grip, but as before it was the man's eyes that captivated her—two dark pools that reflected her own image. 'I am very pleased to make your acquaintance, Dr Rawlings,' he murmured, bending his head slightly over their clasped hands in a sort of formal bow.

'And I yours, Dr Nahum,' she replied.

'Please, my name is Omar.'

'And mine is Sandie.'

'I want Dr Omar,' wailed Gemma suddenly. They all looked down at the little girl and smiled. Omar at last released Sandie's hands then crouched down beside his small patient.

'Hello, Gemma,' he said softly. 'How are you today?'

'That lady had a cup of tea,' said Gemma, staring at Sandie.

'Did she now?' Omar smiled, revealing very white teeth. 'Can I have one, too?'

'It's all gone,' said Gemma solemnly, 'but I can make some more.'

'Good girl,' Omar replied. 'I'll be back.' As he straightened up he opened his hand and in passing caught Lewis's hand, also open in readiness, in a form of greeting. 'Hiya, Tiger,' he said.

The little boy's delight was obvious and as they moved away Penny murmured in Sandie's ear, 'You can see why they adore him, can't you?'

'Absolutely,' she murmured back. 'I can see I shall have to work extra hard in future—the competition seems to be in a league of its own.'

The real work began then as they started to discuss each child's treatment, medication and progress. Lewis was halfway through his course of chemotherapy. 'He's quite sick in the mornings,' said Penny.

'In that case, we could increase his anti-emetic drugs,' replied the oncologist.

'I'll write him up for some,' said Omar, making notes on a pad he took from the pocket of his white coat.

'What about Gemma?' asked Matt. 'Do we have her test results?'

'Bloods and sugars—yes, here they are.' Penny passed the appropriate forms to Matt. 'But we don't have the barium-meal result yet.'

'Well, we'll wait until we have that until we decide anything further,' said Matt as he studied the forms. They moved on from one child to the next, from the girl with Crohn's disease to the child with cystic fibrosis and all the others, assessing each situation, adjusting medication and reviewing treatment where necessary, and by the time they had completed the ward round, Sam Wallis had been admitted to the ward.

'Sam is on your theatre list for later today,' Penny explained to the orthopaedic surgeon.

'Ah, yes,' the surgeon replied, 'this is the young man who was in the road traffic accident.'

'We have him sedated and his pain is controlled,' said Omar.

'And these are Sam's parents.' Penny turned to the couple sitting beside their son. The woman looked distraught, her eyes red from weeping, while her husband appeared gaunt and haggard.

'He will be all right, won't he?' Gill Wallis implored the doctors, her gaze darting from one to another.

'We are going to do our best to make him as good as new again,' the surgeon replied.

'Will he come back here after his operation?' asked the boy's father anxiously.

'Yes.' It was Matt who answered. 'He will be in our care and you can be sure that with Sister Wiseman and her team he will receive the best possible nursing.'

As the consultants moved on and prepared to leave the ward, Sandie lingered to talk to the Wallises.

'He looks so still and so white,' said Gill, staring down at her son.

'That's because he's sedated,' Sandie replied. 'At least this way you know he isn't in any pain.'

'Yes, I suppose so,' Gill replied. 'But he has so many injuries, Doctor, I can't see how they can put everything right for him.'

'You'd be amazed what they can do,' Sandie replied. 'The orthopaedic team we have here at Ellie's is second to none—honestly, they really are superb,' she added when she saw Gill Wallis's doubtful expression. 'About a year ago we had a patient—a teenager who had almost every bone in his body broken from a fall from scaffolding. They put him right and after several months of careful nursing and physiotherapy he has now returned to work.'

'I'd like to get my hands on the person who hit Sam,' said Gary Wallis, staring helplessly down at his son.

'That wouldn't do any good,' said Gill. 'Besides, we don't know exactly what happened yet, do we?'

'What are you saying?' Gary turned sharply on his wife. 'That it was his fault? Is that what you're saying?'

'We don't know,' said Gill. 'We only know he had his football with him—'

'Yes, but he knows better than to play with it on the main road. I've told him time and time again—'

'Listen,' said Sandie, 'it's going to be some little time before Sam goes to Theatre, so why don't the two of you go and get yourselves a coffee or something in the cafeteria?'

'I don't want to leave him,' said Gill stubbornly. 'You can go if you like,' she added, with barely more than a glance in her husband's direction.

'In that case,' said Sandie as Gary stood up, 'you could bring a drink back for Gill.'

Without another word Gary walked out of the ward.

'This is his fault,' said Gill when he was out of earshot. 'He was supposed to take Sam to school this morning, but he let him go on his own, or rather with his mates.'

'So you will know how dreadful he must be feeling now,' said Sandie. 'Think how you would be feeling if you had made that decision.'

'I wouldn't have let him go on his own,' retorted Gill.

'Maybe not today,' said Sandie, 'but the day would have come when you would have had to let him go. Accidents happen at any time.'

'Yes, I suppose so...' Gill lowered her head and without another word Sandie gently touched her shoulder before moving on to the office.

Matt had gone now, together with the other consultants, leaving only Omar with Penny. They both looked up as she came into the room. 'Is everything all right with the Wallises?' asked Penny.

'Yes, I think so,' Sandie replied. 'A bit of blame-apportioning going on but that's pretty well par for the course in these situations.'

'Who's blaming whom?' asked Omar, turning to look through the glass partition to where Gill could be seen sitting alone by her son's bed, her head on her arm.

'She's blaming him,' Sandie replied. 'Apparently he was supposed to take Sam to school but he let him go with his mates— sounds like there was a football involved. I've tried to talk to her—let her see that these things happen and that her husband must be going through hell.'

'The boy's injuries are pretty extensive,' mused Omar.

'But there isn't any reason why he shouldn't make a full recovery, surely?' Sandie's eyes widened slightly.

'Well, we hope not.' Omar turned and looked at her. 'I am on standby at the moment to go down to the special care baby unit where a premature birth is imminent. I would like you to accompany me, please.' His speech and manners were impeccable but there was a hint of something else in those dark eyes as he inclined his head slightly in her direction, although she couldn't for the life of her put her finger on what it was. 'You have your pager with you?'

'Yes, of course,' she replied.

'Then I will page you at the appropriate time,' he replied. Turning slightly, he gave his customary little half-bow in Penny's direction. 'Sister,' he said, then strolled out of the office, pausing only to speak to Lewis and Gemma before leaving the ward.

'He's lovely, isn't he?' said Penny with a little sigh. 'All that old-world charm together with those smouldering looks. And did you see the way he looked at you?'

'What do you mean?' demanded Sandie.

'Well, he can't resist a pretty face—we know that for a fact. And let's face it, he has only just met you. All I can say is that it's a good job you're spoken for, Sandie, otherwise there might be yet another broken heart to contend with.' She paused and peered at Sandie. 'Speaking of which,' she said, 'how is Jon?'

'Jon is fine,' replied Sandie, her voice softening slightly.

'Did you get to see more of him in Manchester than you do down here in Sussex?'

'Yes, I did. He's at a hospital in Chester at the moment so we managed to spend time together—when we weren't working, that is. My schedule was pretty exhausting and Jon works very long hours but, yes, there were times when we were both free.'

'So have the pair of you set a date yet?' asked Penny curiously.

'No, not yet,' Sandie replied lightly.

'Oh, Sandie.' Penny stared searchingly at her and Sandie found herself having to adopt an air of nonchalance, afraid that Penny, who knew her very well, might detect there was something wrong. She didn't want to as much as hint at that for it was something that she had barely yet admitted, even to herself.

'Oh,' she said, 'you know what Jon's like. No one can actually pin him down to anything, but we'll get around to it one day.'

'How long is it now that you've been seeing each other?' Penny obviously wasn't going to let the matter drop.

'Oh, for as long as I can remember,' said Sandie with a laugh. 'Our parents are friends, we went through school together—right from the start we were going to be doctors, then get married and have lots of children. Well, we've achieved the doctor bit but I think the babies will take a bit longer...'

'And presumably the wedding?' said Penny dryly.

'You sound like my mother,' protested Sandie with another laugh. 'Or Jon's mother,' she added darkly. 'They are both desperate for grandchildren.'

'Well, let's hope they won't be disappointed,' said Penny. 'Is Jon planning to come down at all?' She sounded casual but Sandie suddenly had the feeling that she had detected that all was not well.

'Yes.' Sandie nodded. 'Kate and Tom included him on the invitation to their wedding. Wasn't that a wonderful surprise?' she added, in an attempt to draw the conversation away from her relationship with Jon.

'It certainly was,' Penny agreed. 'Who would have thought it? They'd known each other all that time and then suddenly something clicked.'

'I don't think it would have happened before,' said Sandie, 'with Kate still getting over the death of her husband.'

'And from what I've heard, Tom was very wary of commitment following his divorce, which just goes to show there really does have to be a right time for these things to happen.'

'A moment of truth, you mean?' asked Sandie.

'Yes, if you like, or maybe even simply a moment of realisation.'

As Penny bustled back onto the ward Sandie found herself wondering if the same was true in reverse—whether or not there was a moment of truth or realisation when one knew a relationship had ended. Then she gave herself a little shake. Why was she thinking in that way? Her relationship with Jon wasn't over— far from it. Maybe some small aspect of it had changed, although she wasn't even sure about that because it had been so slight, so inconsequential that she was even now wondering whether or not she had imagined it. Maybe things would be better when Jon came down for the wedding.

Her pager sounded at that moment and drove all further thoughts of Jon from her mind. Picking up the phone, she dialled the internal number. Omar answered almost immediately. 'Sandie?' he said, and for some obscure reason, which she was at a total loss to explain—unless it was because of the way he'd said her name with the emphasis on the second syllable instead of the first as everyone else said it—her heart skipped a beat. Not waiting for her to answer, he said, 'We have an imminent birth. Will you join me, please?'

'Of course,' she replied, a little shakily.

CHAPTER TWO

THE baby was tiny, so very tiny. In the end a Caesarean section had been needed and Sandie had scrubbed up alongside Omar before the two of them had gone into Theatre. Tom Fielding, the consultant obstetrician, was delivering the baby and his wife-to-be, Kate, was part of the back-up team. Sandie found herself watching the pair of them as she and Omar stood back until the moment they would be needed. She had been delighted when she had received the invitation to their wedding, as she had said to Penny, but it had certainly been a surprise. She had worked alongside both of them for some considerable time and to her knowledge there had never been the slightest indication of any romance. Had it really been as Penny had said—a moment of realisation? If it had, then that in itself was somehow more intensely romantic than a studied wooing with chocolates and flowers. But, on the other hand, both Kate and Tom were older and this for them was love the second time around. Kate, Sandie knew, had been devastated when her husband had been killed, while Tom had seemed to withdraw deeper and deeper into himself after his divorce.

'You are very, very deep in thought.' A voice suddenly broke into her thoughts and, glancing sideways, she found that Omar was studying her intently.

'Oh,' she said, 'I'm sorry.' She flushed at the intensity of his scrutiny then spoke softly so as not to distract the operating team. 'I was thinking about Mr Fielding and Kate and about them getting married.'

'You approve?' he asked in the same soft tone.

'Oh, yes, although it isn't for me to approve or disapprove. But, yes, I think it's very romantic.'

'So you approve of romance?'

'Of course,' she replied lightly. 'Doesn't everyone?'

There was no time for his response for at that moment the baby was delivered and their presence immediately required. As soon as the cord had been cut and the young mother, who had elected to have an epidural and had therefore been conscious during the operation, had seen and touched her baby, Kate passed the newborn to Sandie.

Quickly she bore the still, tiny form to the far side of the theatre. 'What do we have?' asked Omar.

'A boy,' Sandie replied, then set about clearing the baby's airways of mucus. The infant appeared to be suffering difficulty in breathing, so Sandie moved a respirator forward which she and Omar set up together. When, at last, the baby was breathing by means of the respirator, Omar invited Sandie to carry out a full examination. With a carefully warmed stethoscope Sandie examined the tiny chest and abdomen, detecting a small but distinct heart murmur. Then methodically she tested each little limb, checking for any displacements or abnormalities, and after weighing and measuring the baby she placed him in a specially prepared incubator.

'Let his mum and dad see him before he goes to Special Care,' said Omar as Sandie at last stood back.

Carefully Sandie wheeled the incubator across the theatre to where the baby's parents waited anxiously to see him. They looked so apprehensive that Sandie's heart went out to them as she imagined them having to cope with such a premature baby.

'Here he is,' she said cheerfully, 'all present and correct.'

'What's that tube for?' demanded the baby's father.

'That is to help him breathe.' It was Omar who replied, Omar who had followed Sandie across the theatre and was now standing beside her as she presented the baby to his parents.

'I want to hold him,' said the woman.

Sandie glanced at Omar who shook his head. 'Sorry,' she said, 'not at the moment. We have to get him down to Special Care, but you will both be able to go down there and see him just as soon as Mr Fielding has finished here.'

'How much does he weigh?' asked the baby's mother, as Sandie would have turned away.

'He's just on two pounds,' Sandie replied, whereupon the young woman burst into tears.

They left after that, she and Omar, together with the baby in his incubator, and accompanied by a nurse from the special care baby unit.

Louise, who had obviously been forewarned by the theatre team, was waiting to receive them at the unit.

'A little boy, I understand,' she said. 'Does he have a name yet?'

'Yes.' Sandie glanced at the tag around the baby's minute ankle. 'Augustus Collingwood.'

'Such a grand name for such a tiny little chap,' said Louise with a smile. 'Does he have many problems?'

'His lungs are very underdeveloped,' Omar replied. 'And Sandie detected a heart murmur.'

'We'll put him straight into the high-dependency unit.'

'I'll write him up for medication,' said Omar, 'and, Sandie, perhaps you would arrange for the cardiologist to examine him.'

By the time baby Augustus was settled in the high-dependency unit—a small room with a mass of highly sophisticated equipment—and the consultant cardiologist had been to examine him, word came from Obstetrics that his parents were desperate to visit him.

'Mother was terribly anxious to hold him,' said Sandie.

'That won't be possible at the moment,' Louise replied, 'but we can let her touch him. Do you think that will suffice?'

'I don't know.' Sandie shook her head. 'She seemed rather highly strung and emotional. I'll stay around for a while, if you like.'

'Thanks,' Louise replied. 'People do like to have a doctor around in these circumstances.'

'Omar's still here, isn't he?' Sandie glanced across to Louise's office as she spoke where the top of Omar's head could be seen as he sat at the desk writing up reports.

'Yes, he is but he'll go as soon as he's finished.' Louise paused then, lowering her voice, she added, 'How are you getting on with him?'

'All right—I think.' Sandie shrugged. 'I haven't spent much time with him yet but he seems OK.' What she didn't, couldn't add was that there was definitely something about the new registrar that made her wary. What it was she didn't really know and even if she'd been pressed she wasn't at all sure that she could have said what it was. Unless it was something to do with his sense of self-assurance—maybe even bordering on arrogance, especially where his effect on women was concerned.

Almost as if she could read her thoughts, Louise spoke again. 'He's broken a few hearts already,' she said in the same low tone Sandie had used.

'So I understand,' Sandie replied wryly, 'but you need have no worries in that direction where I am concerned. This heart is intact and I mean to see that it stays that way.'

'Good for you,' Louise replied. She glanced towards the entrance. 'Oh, looks like this little chap's visitors have arrived.'

The baby's parents had indeed arrived—his mother in a wheelchair, accompanied by her husband—together with a nurse from the post-natal ward. They were shown into the high-dependency bay where once again there was near hysteria from Suki Collingwood when she caught sight of her baby and the mass of tubes and equipment that surrounded him. Somehow, between them, Sandie and Louise managed to calm her down sufficiently so that first she, and then her husband Leroy, could reach into the incubator where their baby lay and gently stroke his tiny arms. Apart from the respirator, the baby was linked to a heart monitor, and Omar had inserted a nasogastric tube, which would carry not only nourishment but also medication vital to the baby's survival.

'When can I hold him?' The tears, unchecked, ran freely down Suki's cheeks.

'Maybe in a few days,' Sandie replied. 'When he is a little stronger.'

'Yes,' Louise added, 'and then you will be able to come in and help to care for him—you know, change his nappy and wash him as well as help to feed him.'

At that moment Omar came out of the office and joined them. 'I have to tell you,' he said when the young couple looked up at him in alarm, 'that your baby has been seen by a cardiologist—that is, a heart specialist,' he explained when he saw Suki's and Leroy's blank looks.

'Why?' demanded Leroy in obvious alarm. 'What's wrong with him?'

'He has a heart murmur,' Omar replied gently, and Suki broke into fresh wails. 'But you must not upset yourselves too much. This is something that can be dealt with but again we need to wait a while until he is a little stronger before we decide what has to be done.'

'We need to let our families see him,' said Leroy in a sudden flash of assertiveness. 'My mother, Suki's parents, my brothers, my aunts—'

'Wait a moment.' Louise held up one hand. 'The baby's grandparents can certainly visit, provided they are free of any infection, but I'm afraid that is all we permit on the special care unit.'

'But my family will want to come,' persisted Leroy.

'I'm sorry,' said Louise firmly, 'but those are our rules—parents and grandparents only.'

'Doctor...?' Leroy turned to Omar, as if for back-up, but it was Sandie who intervened.

'The more people who visit this ward, the greater the risk of infection,' she said. 'Just think, if someone had a cold or a tummy bug and they brought it onto the ward and passed it on to your baby or any of the others—these little premature babies simply don't have the strength to fight such things and infection could well bring about death.'

Leroy opened his mouth, maybe to argue further, maybe even to agree, but they were never to know because Suki intervened. 'They aren't coming, Leroy,' she said, and her eyes flashed as she spoke. 'I will not allow anyone to bring infection to my baby.'

Leroy remained silent after that but it left no one in any doubt that it was Suki who was the stronger in the relationship, in spite of her highly strung emotions.

Omar left the special care unit shortly after that, called away to yet another crisis, and as the door closed behind him Louise looked at Sandie. 'Did you know he's going out with Amanda Cromer?' she said.

'Yes.' Sandie nodded. 'Penny mentioned it. I gather from that that there's been no reconciliation with her husband.'

'No.' Louise shook her head. 'I feel a bit sorry for her really, in spite of that bossy way of hers. Apparently she was devastated when her husband left her—he went off with her best friend.'

'Yes, I know.' Sandie paused, then added, 'And now she's going out with our Dr Nahum.'

Louise nodded. 'Rumour has it that she asked him out, that he'd hardly noticed her—mind you, I wouldn't put that past her.'

'Hmm. Maybe,' said Sandie, 'but I couldn't imagine Omar being persuaded into anything he didn't want to do.'

'You've reached that conclusion pretty quickly.' Louise raised an eyebrow. 'You only met him today.'

'Yes, I know, and it's only a feeling.' Sandie shrugged. 'Or maybe you'd call it a hunch. Anyway, I'm going to call it a day. I'm shattered.'

'When did you get back from Manchester?' asked Louise.

'Late last night. I haven't had a chance to sort things out yet.'

'In that case, I won't keep you any longer. See you tomorrow.'

'Yes, OK.' Sandie turned to go, then stopped. 'Oh, Louise, one thing,' she said. 'How is Harry?'

'He's great,' said Louise, a smile softening her features at the mention of her son. 'He's into everything, mind you, but he's just at that age.'

'And the apple of his father's eye, no doubt,' Sandie added with a laugh.

'Oh, absolutely. Matt quite simply adores him.'

Home for Sandie was an apartment in Pitt's Place, a large old house on the very outskirts of the Sussex town of Franchester. Set in its own grounds and well away from any main road, the house had for most of its time been the residence of well-to-do country gentlemen, then a small private school and briefly a hotel. In the early 1990s a wealthy property developer had bought it and converted it into eight luxury apartments. The apartments had sold rapidly, two of them to doctors at Ellie's. For many years Sandie had lived either in shared student flats or hospital accommodation so when she had received a substantial legacy in her grandmother's will and had heard that one of the flats at Pitt's Place was for sale, she hadn't hesitated in putting down a deposit and securing a mortgage.

'It's an investment,' she'd told Jon when he had expressed mild surprise that she should be buying instead of renting. 'Quite apart from which it will be wonderful to have my own place instead of sharing.'

'I hope that doesn't mean you've ruled out sharing with me one day,' he'd said. It was the closest he'd come to a proposal.

'Of course not,' she'd said quickly, 'but it will certainly make life pleasanter in the meantime.'

And it had. For Sandie it was pure bliss to come home at the end of each busy, sometimes frantic day at Ellie's, to turn off the main road into the quiet lane that led to Pitt's Place then to sweep through the pair of black wrought-iron gates and up the drive to the forecourt where, in a crunching of shingle, she would park her car alongside those of the other residents and switch off the engine.

Today was no exception and as always before getting out of the car she lingered for a moment, her hands resting on the steering-wheel as she gazed up at the mellow old house as it basked in the late afternoon autumn sunshine. The house was built of grey stone on Georgian lines, square, with rows of symmetrical windows flanking the main entrance. Attractive ivy with shiny red and green leaves crept over part of the walls, its tendrils reaching up high under the eaves to the attic windows that nestled there, while between the entrance and the forecourt lay a terrace bounded by balustrades and a short flight of stone steps.

Sandie at last stepped out of her car and locked it before mounting the steps, walking across the terrace and letting herself into the house. She had missed her apartment while she had been in Manchester. Even though she had been able to see more of Jon, she had missed so many things—the peace and quiet of the old house, and the wonderful sense of independence it had given her since she had moved in. When she had left for Manchester one of the apartments had been for sale after its owners, a retired solicitor and his wife, had left to live in Spain. Idly, as she crossed the beautiful tiled floor of the hallway and began to climb the sweeping staircase, she wondered if the apartment had sold and, if it had, who her new neighbours were. The two fellow members of staff who also owned apartments were Julie Kershaw, a consultant anaesthetist, and Rob Aitken, a registrar in Accident and Emergency. Sandie was only too aware that in the normal course of events her salary would never have allowed her to purchase such a property, and in her heart she knew she would be grateful for her grandmother's generosity for the rest of her life.

She hadn't seen either Julie or Rob the previous evening when she had arrived home. Neither had she caught sight of them, or indeed any of the other occupants of Pitt's Place, when she had left for work that morning. Her own apartment was on the first floor, as were both Julie's and Rob's, together with the one that had been for sale. There was no sound from Julie's apartment as she passed but from Rob's she heard the faint sound of the classical music that he loved so much. She decided she would catch up with them both later, but for the moment she needed a little space to herself. She was tired, and she had much to do after being away for so long.

Her apartment, off the first-floor landing, was situated at the end of a long corridor whose windows caught the best of the afternoon sun, which now lay in bright wedges of light on the crimson carpet. It consisted of a large sitting room with a dining area leading off it; two bedrooms—a double and a smaller single, which Sandie used as a study; a modern and well-equipped kitchen; and a bathroom. Both the sitting room and her bedroom had glorious views over the garden, with its magnificent variety of trees and shrubs, its pond and ornamental fountain, and right across neighbouring fields to the distant downs beyond. Now, in autumn, the colours of the trees had started to turn and the golds, russets and copper were in stark contrast to the deep greens of the conifers or the shiny leaves of the rhododendrons. It was a view that Sandie never tired of and one she had missed while she had been in Manchester, where she had rented a studio flat in hospital accommodation in the very heart of the city.

'Don't you find it too quiet?' Jon had asked her once when they had been discussing accommodation and she had been telling him how much she loved the peace of Pitt's Place. Jon was a party animal who loved to be in the thick of any action and whose own flat in the centre of Chester was a constant hive of activity and the setting for many parties for staff at the hospital where he worked.

'No,' Sandie had replied in answer to his question, 'it isn't too quiet for me. I love it, and if I do feel in need of noise and activity I just stay on at the hospital social club or go into town to one of the bars or clubs.'

The apartment had already been tastefully decorated when Sandie had bought it but she had quickly stamped her personality on it, adding colour to the plain magnolia walls and the large areas of pearl-grey wood panelling. In her bedroom she had used lilac and touches of turquoise and in the sitting room she'd enhanced the beiges, creams and sand colours of the curtains and furnishings with bright splashes of scarlet. She had added few ornaments, two or three framed family photographs, a tall vase of birch twigs and a large glass bowl filled with highly polished pebbles, and on the walls hung a couple of watercolours by a favourite artist.

The first thing she always did on arriving home was to change out of the dark suit and white shirt she invariably wore for work and into something more comfortable, and today was no exception. After a quick shower she pulled on a pair of faded denims and a figure-hugging white top that left her midriff bare. Her hair, damp from the shower, she spiked up with gel instead of smoothing it into the sleek bob she wore for work. Her plan was to unpack the clothes and books she had brought home from Manchester while her meal was cooking then, maybe later, after she had eaten and if she wasn't too tired, she would see if Julie was around for a drink and a chat. She also wanted to phone Jon but she knew he wouldn't be home yet, as he invariably stopped off somewhere on his way home from the hospital. There was still a little niggle somewhere at the back of her mind concerning Jon and the way things were between them, but she still wasn't quite able to put her finger exactly on what it was. Maybe, she thought as she loaded the washing-machine, there wasn't anything wrong at all; maybe it was simply her being silly.

She had just poured herself a glass of wine before starting to prepare her meal when there came a ring at her doorbell. With a little smile and still carrying her wineglass, she hurried to the door. 'You've beaten me to it,' she said, tugging open the door and fully expecting to see Julie there. 'I was going to come down to see you later...' She trailed off, her eyes widening in amazement, for, instead of Julie, Omar Nahum stood in the doorway.

He too was casually dressed, in chinos and a cream sweatshirt and a pair of deck shoes. In one hand he carried a bottle of champagne and in the other what appeared to be a takeaway meal in a white plastic carrier.

For a split second neither of them spoke, Sandie through shock and Omar as if he too was slightly thrown by something. In the end it was he who broke the silence.

'Sandie,' he said, and once again that emphasis was on the second syllable of her name, 'I wanted to welcome you home.'

'Omar,' she said. 'Whatever are you doing here?'

'Like I said...' He gave a little shrug. 'I wanted to welcome you home.'

'Well, that's very kind of you, but I already saw you at work...' She trailed off, uncertain how to continue, aware once again of some depth of emotion in those dark, liquid eyes.

'Ah,' he said, 'but that was then, at the hospital, and this is here, at home.'

'But I don't understand.' She frowned. 'How did you know where I live?'

'Rob told me,' he said.

'Rob—you mean Rob Aitken?' She frowned, unable to fathom why Rob should have told Omar where she lived.

'Yes.' He nodded then looked over her shoulder into her apartment. 'Aren't you going to ask me in?'

'Well…' She hesitated, uncertain what to do. She wasn't at all sure she wanted Omar in her apartment, given his track record where women were concerned, but on the other hand he was her superior and he had apparently come there with the express purpose of welcoming her home, so it might appear rude if she was to send him away without any sort of gesture of hospitality. 'Yes…' she said at last, 'Yes, of course. Please, come in. I'm sorry,' she added as he stepped into her small hallway and she closed the door behind him, 'I was forgetting my manners. You must forgive me—it was just that it was a bit of a shock seeing you here, that's all.'

'That's all right,' he said, following her into the kitchen. 'Have you eaten yet?'

'No, not yet.'

'Good,' he said. 'In that case, maybe you will join me in eating this curry?'

'Oh!' she said, staring at the carrier bag he carried.

'You don't like curry?' He looked concerned.

'I love curry.'

'That's good.' He began to take containers out of the bag, not the usual ones provided by the local Indian take-away but stainless-steel ones with fitted lids.

'Have you been to a take-away?' she asked curiously at last.

'Of course not,' he replied. 'I make this myself. It only needs reheating, but first this.' He held up the bottle of champagne. 'It is beautifully chilled and ready for drinking.'

'It looks like you've thought of everything,' she said weakly.

'Well, I hope I have.' He smiled. His smile really was quite devastating. Sandie could quite see why he had made so much impact on so many members of the female staff.

'I'll get some glasses,' she said, leading the way out of the kitchen into the sitting room.

She had a set of champagne flutes, which had been a present from her parents and which she kept in a glass-fronted cupboard in the Swedish pine dresser in one corner of the sitting room. While she was taking two of the flutes from the cupboard Omar stood for a moment, looking around, then strolled across the room to the large windows that overlooked the garden.

'This is a nice aspect on this side of the house,' he said, 'different from the front.'

'Yes,' she replied, thinking what he had said sounded rather odd. 'It is nice.'

'Let me deal with this cork,' he said, and strolled back to the kitchen.

While he was gone Sandie frantically looked around, wondering what on earth she had done, asking this man into her home. She had only met him that day for the first time. She knew next to nothing about him, apart from the fact that he was a doctor and that he had something of a reputation with women, and here she was about to embark on drinking a bottle of champagne with him—and, if that wasn't enough, to consume food that he himself had prepared and brought to her home on the assumption that she would be eager to share it with him. She had suspected the arrogance of the man—surely this proved her suspicions. What she needed to do was to put a stop to this before it went any further. As Omar came back into the room she swung round to face him.

'Omar,' she began. 'Dr Nahum, I've been thinking—'

But that was as far as he allowed her to go for as he took one of the flutes and half filled first it, then the other, with the foaming, bubbling champagne he said smoothly, 'Tell me, Sandie, how long have you lived here at Pitt's Place?'

'Er, two years, but—'

'Two years—as long as that? And you are happy here?'

'Well, yes...'

'But that is a foolish question. You quite obviously are happy. If you weren't, you wouldn't stay.'

'It suits me,' she said, suddenly on the defensive about her home, imagining some criticism on his part, just as Jon had criticised it when he had first seen it, forcing her to defend both it and her reasons for buying it. 'I know it's quiet here, but that is what I like. It is a peaceful place.'

'You are quite right,' he said handing her a glass. 'It is very peaceful. People nowadays tend to overlook the need for peace in their busy, humdrum lives. What they don't realise is that it is peace that restores balance and allows them to continue. They go on and on until they reach burnout then depression takes over.'

'Well, yes,' she agreed. She looked down at the contents of her glass but before she could think of any comment that might sound in the least bit intelligent he raised his own glass.

'To peace,' he said.

'I'll certainly drink to that,' she said. She took a sip. It was incredibly good champagne but somehow she wasn't surprised. She had already assumed that Omar Nahum was a man who liked the finer things in life.

Suddenly she realised that he was looking around again as if for somewhere to sit. 'Oh, please,' she said, 'do sit down…'

He sat on the sofa while she took an armchair where she sat with one leg curled under her while she sipped the champagne—probably faster than she should have done. Desperately she sought for something to say and was just on the point of asking him where he had worked before coming to Ellie's when he suddenly set his glass down and stared at her.

'You look different,' he said.

'How do you mean, different?' She stared back at him, slightly startled by his scrutiny which seemed to travel from her face and hair to the top she was wearing, her exposed midriff, which she was suddenly acutely conscious of, and her bare feet with their red painted toenails.

'From how you did at work today,' he said at last.

'Well, yes,' she agreed, embarrassed now by the look in his eyes, which was beginning to look suspiciously like admiration. 'I don't wear jeans for work.'

'I wasn't meaning the jeans,' he said. 'I was meaning more your hair…'

Startled, she put one hand to her head and then she remembered how she had spiked up her hair after her shower.

'It's different, but I like it. It suits you.' He paused. 'Smooth and sophisticated for work and fun and sexy off duty.'

Sandie felt her cheeks flame and in order to cover her embarrassment took a large mouthful of champagne. Had he started already—trying to charm her, to get round her just as he had all the others? Well, if he had, she would soon put a stop to it. 'I understand,' she said tilting her head in what she hoped was an assertive manner, 'that you and Amanda Cromer are an item?'

If she had thought he would in any way be fazed by her question she was sadly mistaken for he merely smiled. 'Amanda and I have certainly been out together a few times,' he replied, 'but an item? I'm not really sure what that means.'

'That you are together, recognised as a couple,' she said.

'Ah,' he said, 'I see.' Leaning forward, he refilled her glass. She knew that really she should stop him but somehow she seemed to lack the will to do so. He didn't elaborate any further as to whether or not he saw Amanda and himself as an item and really—possibly

because the champagne was doing its job—
Sandie found she didn't care.

'So what about you?' he said, after he had
refilled his own glass. 'Is there anyone with
whom you would consider yourself to be an
item?'

'Oh, yes,' she said, pulling a face as the
champagne bubbles fizzed in her nose, 'there
is. His name is Jon.'

Omar didn't so much as blink. 'And what
does Jon do?' he asked at last.

'He's a doctor.'

'At Ellie's?' He raised his eyebrows.

'No, not at Ellie's—in Chester.'

'Chester. That's a long way. You can't get
to see each other very often.'

'No,' she agreed. 'We don't.' She reflected
for a moment, staring into her glass. Then,
looking up, she said, 'We did see more of each
other when I was in Manchester.'

'But now you're back home,' he said, glancing around the room.

'Yes,' she replied, 'now I'm back home.'
She paused, looking across the room at him to
where he sat on her sofa, his long legs
stretched out before him and one arm lying

along the back. 'Where do you live? Are you in hospital accommodation?'

He stared at her, and in that moment, for Sandie, everything seemed very still, one of those moments when the world seemed to pause and take a deep breath before turning again. 'No, Sandie,' he said at last, 'I don't live in hospital accommodation. I thought you knew.'

'You thought I knew what?'

'I live here,' he said.

She stared at him, her brain somehow rendered incapable of assimilating what he had said. 'You live here?' she said stupidly at last. 'What do you mean?'

'I live here at Pitt's Place,' he said. 'I bought the apartment next to yours two months ago. I'm your new neighbour.'

CHAPTER THREE

IT TOOK a moment for what Omar had said to sink in, a moment during which Sandie continued to stare at him in astonishment.

'You didn't know?' he said at last.

She shook her head, words still failing her.

'I thought you would have done,' he said.

'How? How would I have known?' At last she managed to speak but her voice came out sounding strange, not like her voice at all.

'I thought maybe Rob or perhaps Julie would have told you.'

'I haven't seen either of them since I got back from Manchester.'

'And you weren't in touch while you were away?' he asked curiously.

'Well, yes, I was. Of course I was—with Julie—to see if everything was all right.'

'And she didn't say anything then?'

Sandie took a deep breath. 'She told me that the apartment had been sold and that the previous owners had left for Spain.'

'But she didn't say anything about the new owner—is that it?'

'I don't know. She may have done—I can't remember.' Sandie began racking her brain to see if she could recall Julie saying anything about their new neighbour being a fellow doctor at Ellie's, but for some reason she found that her mind was a complete blank.

'Well, never mind.' He stood up. 'I'm here now and, like you, I very much enjoy living here. Now, you finish your champagne and I'll go and reheat the curry.'

He disappeared into the kitchen and Sandie heard the click as he opened the door of the microwave. She still could hardly believe what he had just told her—that not only was he going to be working alongside her every day but he would also be living in the next-door apartment. She really wasn't sure how she felt about that. She got on very well with Julie and Rob and even though they all worked at Ellie's they worked in different departments and sometimes hardly saw one another for days at a time. With Omar it would practically be round-the-clock contact and if tonight was anything to go by, it would appear that he thought he

would be able to pop into her apartment whenever the fancy took him.

She would, she thought, have to put a stop
to that or at least let him know that she valued
her privacy and her independence and didn't
like people dropping in as and when they
thought fit. Maybe now was a good time to
say that, before things went too far. If only she
hadn't drunk so much champagne, she thought
as she stood up and the room seemed to tilt
slightly. Taking a deep breath, she headed a
little unsteadily towards the kitchen.

'Oh,' he said, looking over his shoulder, 'I
was hoping not to bother you. You seemed so
relaxed sitting there…'

'I'm not drunk,' she protested angrily.

'Drunk?' He turned then and stared at her.
'Did I say anything about being drunk?'

'No,' she admitted reluctantly, when he appeared to be waiting for an answer, 'but I felt
you implied it.'

'It never crossed my mind,' he replied
smoothly. He paused. 'On the other hand, we
did consume that champagne rather quickly…'

'So are you drunk?' She seized upon the notion, not for one moment believing it to be true.

He smiled, that rather enigmatic smile she had seen before. 'It would,' he said lightly, 'take a little more than that so, no, not drunk, merely pleasantly relaxed. Now...' he looked around the kitchen '...I was looking for plates...'

'Here.' She moved forward and opened a cupboard, taking out two plates.

'Good,' he said, turning back to the microwave. 'The curry is almost ready. Why don't you take the plates and some cutlery and I'll join you in a moment, unless of course you wanted to eat here in the kitchen?' He glanced at the kitchen stools as he spoke.

'No.' She shook her head. 'The dining bay is more comfortable.' Without another word she picked up the plates, took cutlery from a drawer and made her way back through the sitting room to the dining table. So much for her intention of telling him that she wanted her privacy respected, she thought wryly. Well, maybe she would be able to do so later, after they had eaten. It would have to be done tactfully, of course. After all, she grudgingly conceded, he had gone to the trouble of bringing her a meal and when all was said and done she did still have to work alongside him, so the last thing she wanted was any animosity between them.

Moments later he appeared with the dishes of curry on a tray, which he set down in the middle of the table.

'It smells awfully good,' said Sandie, picking up a serving spoon.

It tasted good too, exceptionally good, and in spite of the thoughts and feelings she had been experiencing she found herself thoroughly enjoying the food. The conversation shifted away from them and centred on their work and mutual acquaintances. Omar proved to be not only charming but also entertaining, with a sharp sense of humour and a gift for mimicry which, in spite of her earlier misgivings, had Sandie helpless with laughter.

'Are you going to this wedding next weekend?' he asked at last.

'Yes. Are you?'

'Yes.' He nodded and for some obscure reason she found herself feeling pleased that he was going.

They had almost finished the meal when her phone rang. Excusing herself, Sandie left the table and took the call in the sitting room. It was Jon, and just for one moment she felt a stab of something—she wasn't sure what, but it felt suspiciously like guilt, which was completely and utterly ridiculous. After all, what did she have to feel guilty about? She was merely enjoying supper with a colleague.

'Oh, Jon,' she said. 'Hello.'

'Sandie, sorry, is this a bad time?'

'It is a bit,' she replied, desperately trying to swallow the mouthful of food she had put in her mouth in the second before the phone had rung.

'You're eating,' he said.

'Yes, I am. Could I ring you back later, Jon?'

'Yes, sure, although I do have to go out later.' He paused. 'Are you on your own?'

Sandie couldn't imagine why he had asked her that. He didn't usually ask such questions—maybe he had picked up some inflection in her voice, which indicated she wasn't alone. 'No,' she replied, 'I have...' She hesitated, but only fractionally. 'I have a neighbour here who also happens to work at Ellie's.'

'Oh? Julie or Rob?' he said.

'Neither actually,' she replied. 'It's a new neighbour and a new colleague.'

'Is she a doctor?'

'Registrar actually and...and she's a he,' she added.

There was a brief silence on the other end of the line, then Jon said, 'Right, well, don't let me keep you.'

'OK. Like I said, I'll ring you back later.'

'Yes, all right. Bye, Sandie.'

'Bye, Jon.' She replaced the receiver and walked slowly back into the dining area.

Omar had stopped eating, obviously waiting for her, but as she sat down his dark gaze moved searchingly over her face. 'Was that your boyfriend?' he asked.

'Yes,' she admitted, 'that was Jon. I'm going to ring him back later,' she added unnecessarily.

'How did he feel at you having supper with another man?' There was definitely a gleam of amusement in his eyes now.

'Probably the same as Amanda would feel if she were to phone you now,' she retorted lightly. When he didn't respond, she said, 'On the other hand, you probably wouldn't tell Amanda.'

'Now, what on earth makes you think that?' He looked mildly surprised.

'Because you are a man,' she said simply.

'So are you suggesting that women are more honest about these things?' he asked. Once again that dark gaze was scrutinising her features, moving easily from her eyes to her mouth, to her hair, then back to her eyes, before finally coming to rest on her mouth.

'In my experience, yes,' she answered firmly. But for some reason his scrutiny was doing something to her concentration—something deadly, for she found she was beginning to lose the thread of the conversation.

'Ah,' he said at last, leaning back in his chair, 'interesting. So what did you tell him—your boyfriend? Or is he your fiancé?'

'Not exactly,' Sandie replied. She looked away from him, away from that gaze, trying instead to concentrate on the pattern on the tablecloth. 'I simply told him I was having supper with my new neighbour who also happens to be a colleague.' She didn't say that Jon had assumed the colleague to be female—not that that would have made any difference to Omar, for he seemed more concerned over whether or not Jon was her fiancé.

'What do you mean,' he said, 'not exactly?'

'Well, we've known each other all our lives. Our families have always been friends so as far as they are all concerned it's like we are engaged and it's only a matter of time before we get married.'

'And what about where you and Jon are concerned?'

She glanced up and the gaze was as intense as ever, almost as if he could see into the depths of her very soul. 'The same really…' she said at last, but her reply sounded less than convincing, even to herself. 'It's been difficult,' she went on after a moment, as if she felt compelled in some way to defend their position, 'what with Jon working in Chester and me down here in Sussex...'

'Have neither of you never attempted to find work nearer to the other?' There was mild curiosity in his voice now.

'Well, Jon wanted me to go up there once— there was a post going at his hospital...'

'And?' He lowered his head slightly in order to be able to look into her face again.

'I felt it to be a backward step, career-wise,' she said. 'The post I had here at Ellie's was far better.'

'And was he, Jon, upset about this?'

'Yes, I suppose he was,' she said, reflecting briefly on how Jon had accused her of not wanting to sacrifice her job for the sake of their relationship. 'But later the situation was reversed when a post came up here at Ellie's and he refused to apply for it for similar reasons. The situation hasn't arisen since and we've just, well, just...'

'Drifted along?' Omar asked, raising one eyebrow.

'Well, yes, I suppose so, although I wouldn't really have put it quite like that. You make it sound as if there is no spark left, that the relationship has exhausted itself...'

'And it hasn't?' he asked.

'No, of course not,' she protested. 'Why, while I was in Manchester we saw a lot of each other.'

'I'm sure you did.' Omar nodded then after an almost imperceptible pause he said, 'So did it move things along in any way, spending all this time together?'

'What do you mean?' Sandie frowned, uncertain where this particular conversation was leading.

'Well, did you not get around to discussing wedding plans? Isn't that what prospective brides like to do?'

'No, we didn't,' she said flatly. 'Once again, the job situation would be the main barrier against us getting together.' Somehow she couldn't bring herself to admit to this man who seemed to have the uncanny knack of knowing what was going on inside her head that Jon had never actually proposed to her, in spite of all the assumptions from their respective families.

'I see.' He paused and the silence was infinitely more eloquent than any words. 'Tell me,' he said at last, 'will Jon be with you for Tom and Kate's wedding?'

'Yes,' Sandie replied relieved to talk about something else, 'yes, he will. It'll only be a fleeting visit but, yes, he's coming down.'

He went soon after that, refusing Sandie's offer of coffee saying he was sure she had things to do. Which, of course, she had, so why was it, in spite of her earlier reluctance to allow him in, and her slight irritation about his questioning of her over Jon, that she felt a tinge of regret when he refused the coffee and left her to go back to his own apartment?

It felt very empty after he had gone. She'd seen him to the door and thanked him for the food and the champagne. 'You'll have to let me cook something another time.' Had she really said that? And had his eyes lit up at the prospect or had she imagined it?

'Goodnight, Sandie,' he'd said, and his voice had been low, soft, like a caress.

After he had gone she didn't feel like doing any of the jobs she had intended doing but the one thing she knew she had to do was to phone Jon.

The phone rang several times before he answered. 'I was just on my way out,' he said.

'Sorry,' she said. 'Do you have to go immediately?'

'No, it's OK. Has your friend gone?'

'He isn't really a friend,' she said. 'Like I said, he's bought the apartment next door—you know, the one where the couple went to Spain. He also happens to be a registrar at Ellie's. I met him at work today for the first time, not knowing that he had an apartment here at Pitt's Place.'

'So what happened—did he invite himself to supper?'

'Sort of. He arrived at the door with a curry.'

'Bit odd, that, wasn't it?'

'Well, not really. It was by way of a welcome home, and in all fairness he thought I knew he was my new neighbour.' Somehow she couldn't bring herself to mention the champagne.

'So what's his name?'

She was faintly surprised at Jon's persistence. He didn't usually question her in this way over her friends or who she chose or did not choose to spend her time with. 'It's Dr Nahum,' she replied, 'Omar Nahum.'

'Indian or Pakistani?' he asked.

'Neither. Apparently his mother is English but his father is from somewhere in Africa—Sudan or Somalia or somewhere. I can't really remember. Anyway, Omar himself is very British. You'll meet him when you come down for the wedding.'

'Yes, right.' Jon sounded less than enthralled at the prospect and Sandie felt a little rush of annoyance. She always tried to take an interest in his life, his friends and his work. Surely it wasn't too much to expect for him to do the same for her. They talked for only a short time longer, about quite inconsequential matters, then Jon said he really would have to be going, they said goodnight and hung up.

Sandie still felt vaguely irritated as she prepared for bed, especially when it dawned on her that Jon hadn't actually told her where he was dashing off to in such a hurry. All he had seemed concerned with was the fact that she had been having supper in her apartment with a man he didn't know. Briefly she found herself wondering how she would have felt had Jon told her he had been having supper with a woman friend whom she didn't know, and she realised that she really didn't know how she would have felt. She wasn't at all certain that she would have been jealous. She and Jon had known each other for so long, knew practically everything there was to know about each other, and somehow jealousy simply wasn't an emotion that had ever come into their relationship.

She wondered about this even after she'd climbed into bed and lay staring up at the ceiling. Did it say something about the nature of their relationship that she didn't feel any jealousy? Was Jon jealous of what she did? Had he felt jealous tonight? She was no nearer finding answers to her questions when at last she drifted off to sleep but intriguingly, in those last moments before sleep claimed her, her thoughts were not of Jon but of Omar and those dark eyes of his which had seemed capable of looking right into her soul.

*　　*　　*

'Gemma's test results are back.' Penny passed the forms to Sandie, who studied them carefully.

'Matt's not here today,' she replied slowly. 'I'd better let Omar have these.'

'Gemma's parents are here.' Penny glanced into the ward.

'Both of them?' Sandie looked up in surprise. 'I thought they didn't have contact with each other.'

'Well, I don't think they do under normal circumstances,' Penny replied, 'but I guess these aren't exactly normal circumstances.'

'No, quite,' Sandie agreed. 'Were they ever married?' she asked as an afterthought.

Penny shook her head. 'No. Justin Woods left Gemma's mother, Gaby, soon after Gemma was born. He sees Gemma on a fairly regular basis but that is arranged through Gemma's grandmother.' She paused. 'What do the tests say?'

'It looks like her problem is with the enzymes that digest her food.'

'That would explain why she isn't able to keep anything down,' Penny replied. 'Would you have a look at Lewis as well, please?' she went on after a moment. 'He's not very bright this morning—very lethargic, in fact. And Sam Wallis needs more pain relief.' She glanced at her watch. 'Omar should be here in about half an hour—he phoned to say he's in a meeting but that you would hold the fort until he gets here.'

'That's very good of him,' Sandie replied dryly. Glancing at Penny, she added, 'I wish you'd told me about him, Penny.'

'What about him?' Penny threw her a puzzled look as the two of them left her office and walked out onto the ward.

'Well, that he'd bought an apartment in the same place as me.'

'Oh, Sandie, I'm sorry.' Penny paused and stared at her. 'I thought you would have known. I thought Julie would have told you.'

'I saw Julie this morning before I left for work and she swears that she did tell me on the phone, but I honestly don't have any recollection of it.'

'So when did you find out?'

'Last night,' Sandie replied wryly, 'when Omar appeared on my doorstep, complete with champagne and curry by way of a welcome home.'

Penny's eyes widened in amazement then she chuckled. 'Oh, he really is lovely, isn't he?'

'Well, yes, I suppose…but I still wish I'd been forewarned…'

'So you had a cosy supper with the delectable Dr Nahum… Mmm.' Penny purred appreciatively. 'Can't be bad. Just one thing, though,' she added. 'You'd better not let Amanda find out about it—I've heard she's very possessive where Omar is concerned.'

'Well, I can assure you, she has nothing to worry about from me. And besides, I have Jon…'

'Yes, of course,' said Penny. 'I was forgetting. How silly of me. Still, it was kind of Omar, wasn't it?'

'Yes,' Sandie was forced to agree, 'yes, I suppose it was.'

The children's ward at Ellie's was always busy and that particular morning was no exception. A radio provided background music while the staff struggled to maintain some sort of routine, whether it was feeding the children, seeing to their medical care or washing and dressing those who weren't on bed rest. Sandie went to Sam Wallis first. The curtains were drawn around the boy's bed and when she opened them a few inches and peered in it was to find that Staff Nurse Emma Hollingsworth and nursery nurse Kimberly Graham had just finished giving the boy a bed bath. The boy's left leg was in plaster and his shoulder and left arm were supported in a sling. He was obviously in some pain and discomfort from being moved. His parents, Gill and Gary, were seated nearby. Both seemed upset by their son's distress.

'Can't you do anything to help him?' demanded Gary as soon as he caught sight of Sandie.

'That's what I'm here for,' Sandie replied, taking the boy's observation chart from the end of his bed and studying it. 'What sort of night has he had?' she asked, half turning to Penny.

'Very restless,' Penny replied. 'His temperature was up slightly but it's normal again now. He was also very sick this morning.'

'I'll write him up for something for the sickness,' Sandie replied, 'and I'll increase his pain relief.' Moving round the side of the bed, she took hold of Sam's hand. 'Hello, Sam,' she said. The boy moved his head, looked at her, then turned his face to the wall. 'We'll soon have you feeling a lot better,' she said gently, as Emma drew back the curtains and the morning sunshine flooded in. 'There,' she said, 'that's better already—at least we can see you properly now.' Still the boy's face remained resolutely turned away.

'Did everything go well with the operation?' Gary stood up as Sandie moved away from the bed.

'Didn't you see the surgeon afterwards?' she asked, her gaze moving from Gary to his wife then back again.

He shook his head. 'No, it was very late when they finished and he apparently left straight away.'

'There weren't any complications, were there, Sister?' Sandie glanced at Penny.

'Not as far as I know,' Penny replied. 'But Dr Nahum, the registrar, will be round shortly—you can speak to him if you are at all worried. Failing that, the consultants will be doing a ward round later this morning.'

'Looks like we'll just have to wait until then.' Gary gave a helpless gesture.

'Well, we aren't going anywhere, are we?' said Gill. She spoke in a resigned sort of voice, as if she'd done so much waiting already that a little longer wasn't going to make too much difference. 'Unless...' she threw her husband a withering glance '...you were planning to go back to work.'

'No,' he muttered, 'of course I wasn't.'

Sandie, sensing increased tension between Sam's parents, made her way back to Penny's office where she wrote up the new medication that was required for the boy. She had almost finished when she sensed someone watching her. Looking up quickly from the desk, she found Omar standing in the doorway and she suddenly had the strange feeling that he had been there for some time.

'Oh,' she said, feeling the colour rush to her cheeks and hating herself for it, wishing she could appear merely cool and in complete control instead of off guard and harassed. 'I didn't know you were there.'

'It's all right,' he said softly. 'I could see you were busy, I was merely waiting until you had finished.'

'I...I was just writing Sam Wallis up for more pain relief.'

'How is he this morning?'

'Not very happy.' Sandie shook her head. 'He's in pain and he has been sick so I included an anti-emetic in his medication.'

'Good.' Omar leaned across her to pick up the folder containing Sam's notes, and as he did so Sandie caught the scent of his aftershave, a slightly musky, rather sensual smell, and felt herself give an involuntary little shiver.

'His parents are anxious to talk to someone about the operation,' she said after a moment.

'Haven't they spoken to the orthopaedic surgeon?' Omar frowned.

'No, not yet. It seems the operation was very late last night and there was no opportunity.'

'In that case, I'll be happy to talk to them.'

'There weren't any complications, were there?' asked Sandie as Omar continued to read the theatre report.

'Not really. The boy is young and healthy and the femur and the clavicle should heal well. He does, however, have a pin in his pelvis—that may take a bit longer, but I'll go and have a word with them. I see from this that his temperature was raised for a time.'

'Yes.' Sandie nodded. 'But it's normal again now.'

'If it goes up again we may need to think about antibiotics.' Omar paused and closed the folder. 'Now, is there anything else?' he asked.

'Gemma's test results are back,' Sandie replied.

'Ah, I shall be interested to see those.'

Sandie rummaged through the pile of folders on Penny's desk, found Gemma's then extricated the appropriate form, which she handed to Omar.

'Any thoughts on this?' he asked after a moment of study.

'I think we are looking at an enzyme problem,' Sandie replied.

'My thoughts exactly,' he replied. 'We need Matt to see this then maybe we can get this little girl on the right form of treatment. Now, is there anything else I need to know about this morning?'

'Well, apparently Lewis is rather lethargic. My next task was to go and see him.'

'All right.' Omar nodded. 'Let me know if there is a problem—it's probably just a side effect of his chemotherapy, but we need to make sure.'

Sandie stood up, expecting Omar to move out of the office into the ward so that she could follow him as there was barely room for the two of them to pass in the tiny office, but instead he continued to stand there with his back to the door. 'Omar…?' she said at last, when still he showed no signs of moving.

'I enjoyed last night,' he said softly, and once again to Sandie's consternation that deeply searching expression was back in his eyes, those eyes so dark they appeared almost black.

For a moment he so took her by surprise she didn't know what to say. The last thing she had expected had been for him to refer to what had happened the night before, especially in the middle of a busy ward routine. But as he waited it became obvious that he wanted some sort of response from her on the subject.

'Yes,' she heard herself say, 'I enjoyed it as well. It was…nice.'

'Only nice?' He raised his eyebrows.

'Well…' She floundered for something else to say, something that wouldn't sound as if she was ungrateful but which at the same time wouldn't sound completely over the top.

'Nice is a strange word,' he said, 'a very lukewarm adjective which never adequately describes any situation, especially one as enjoyable as last night.'

'Well, no, maybe not,' she agreed. 'Maybe your choice of word is better—it was enjoyable.'

He laughed then, revealing his very white teeth. 'That's better,' he said. 'You had me thinking that maybe I shouldn't have done what I did…'

'Oh, no,' she said quickly, 'nothing like that. It was very kind of you…and…and it was very much appreciated.' Somehow she still seemed to be having difficulty finding the right words.

'So, did you make your phone call after I'd gone?'

'My phone call?' Stupidly she gazed at him, wondering what he meant.

'Yes, to your boyfriend?' he said. There was a half-smile on his face now as his gaze came to rest on her mouth.

'Oh, that. Yes,' she said, 'I did. I called Jon before I went to bed.'

'What was his reaction?' He was still looking at her mouth and suddenly Sandie began to feel very uncomfortable, a hot sort of feeling rising from the pit of her stomach.

'I don't understand…' she said.

'Well, I can't imagine he was exactly enthralled to learn that his girlfriend had been enjoying supper and champagne with another man, so much so that she chose not to speak to him when he called and elected to call him back at a more convenient time.'

'He was OK.' She shook her head impatiently. How dared this man question her in this way? Who did he think he was? 'He quite understood that what you did was simply a kindly gesture from a new neighbour who also happens to be a colleague,' she added stiffly.

'And the champagne?' he said softly, his gaze moving from her mouth to her eyes again. 'Did he understand that was just a kindly gesture as well?'

'Actually,' she retorted, 'I didn't mention the champagne.' She could have kicked herself as soon as she'd said it, but it was too late and he seized upon it.

'Ah,' was all he said, but it was enough.

'Not that I was deliberately trying to conceal anything,' she went on hotly.

'No,' he said smoothly, 'of course not. But I think it was probably very wise not to mention it, especially as we did consume it rather quickly. I'm not sure how I would have reacted if my girlfriend had told me she had just drunk a bottle of champagne with a man she hardly knew. On the other hand, I would probably never leave any girlfriend of mine alone long enough for that to happen.'

She stared at him. 'I told you about that, about why Jon and I are apart.'

'Oh, yes,' he said, 'yes, of course you did. I forgot. It's all down to your jobs.' He moved then, opening the door to allow them both to go back onto the ward, but as Sandie was forced to brush past him, so close that fleetingly she felt his breath on her cheek, he spoke once more, again very softly but loud enough so there could be no mistake over what he said. 'If you were my woman, Sandie,' he murmured, 'something would have to change, because whatever the circumstances I would have to have you right there beside me.'

CHAPTER FOUR

SANDIE was glad to immerse herself in the demands of the ward once more but if she'd been aware of Omar before, she was even more aware of him now. There had been something intensely intimate in those few, softly spoken words when he had suggested what it would be like for him if she were his woman. Working in hospital environments, as she had for several years Sandie had heard more than her fair share of chat-up lines and could usually give the flippant dismissal most of them called for, but somehow she doubted this had been a chat-up line. For a start, she didn't imagine that Omar needed to engage in chat-up lines—he was, after all, already in a relationship of his own, just as he was fully aware of her own circumstances. On the other hand, hadn't she been warned right from the start that he had a reputation as a heartbreaker?

Maybe he was simply running true to form and she needed to heed the warning signs.

Once back on the ward she made a concentrated effort to pull herself together and get on with the job in hand. She decided she'd ignore any further advances on Omar's part, if indeed that was what they were, and she wasn't wholly convinced of that. Maybe he quite simply treated all women that way.

There seemed to be some sort of dispute going on between Gemma's parents while the little girl played her favourite game in the Wendy house, apparently oblivious to what was going on around her.

'Is there a problem?' asked Sandie as the argument grew increasingly louder, attracting the attention of Sam's parents and of others further down the ward.

'I want me girlfriend to come and see Gemma.' Justin Woods, with his shaved head and numerous skin piercings, which included an eyebrow and his nose quite apart from the more usual loops in both earlobes, rounded on Sandie. 'This slag says she can't.'

'She's the slag, not me,' shrieked Gemma's
mother. 'She ain't coming anywhere near my
daughter.'

'You can't stop her,' yelled Justin. 'This is
a public place—anyone can come in.'

'It also happens to be a hospital,' said
Sandie. 'There are very sick children on this
ward and if you don't stop this noise immediately I'll be forced to call Security and you'll
be asked to leave.'

'You've no right to do that.' Justin took a
threatening step towards Sandie and just for a
moment her nerve almost failed her, but she
needn't have worried for Omar, who must
have been watching what was going on from
further down the ward, was quite suddenly at
her side.

'Yes, she does,' he said. 'She has every
right, and I'll thank you not to intimidate Dr
Rawlings or any other member of staff.'

'I ain't done nuffink,' said Justin, but his
aggression seemed to shrink under Omar's
steady gaze. 'All I said was I wanted me girlfriend to come and see Gemma—it's her
what's causing all the trouble,' he muttered,

jerking his thumb in Gaby's direction, 'cos she said she can't come.'

'At the moment it is best for Gemma if we keep her visitors to parents and grandparents,' said Omar. He spoke quietly but his voice was full of authority. For one awful moment Sandie thought Justin was going to square up to him but instead his shoulders slumped and he sat down again in the chair beside the Wendy house.

'Yeah, all right,' he muttered. Then, his eyes suddenly narrowing, he squinted up at Omar and Sandie. 'Have you found out somefink else about Gemma?' he demanded suspiciously, 'somefink you ain't tellin' us?'

'We have Gemma's test results back,' replied Omar in the same quiet, authoritative tones.

'What are they?' This time it was Gaby on her feet, her forehead creased with anxiety, her eyes wide with apprehension. 'What's wrong with her?'

'Well, we know from the tests that Gemma has difficulty keeping her food down—' Sandie began.

'We know that!' snorted Justin. 'Tell us somefink we don't know!'

'This is because there is a problem with one of the substances which helps to digest her food.' Smoothly Omar carried on talking as if Justin hadn't interrupted.

'What is this substance?' demanded Gaby.

'It's called an enzyme,' Omar explained.

'So what you goin' to do about it, then?' said Justin.

'Well, now that we know exactly what it is that is causing this problem,' Omar replied, 'we can start Gemma on the proper course of treatment. We need to talk to Dr Forrester first—'

'Today?' demanded Gaby.

'No, not today,' Sandie intervened. 'Dr Forrester isn't here today.'

'Where is he, then?' Justin began to look belligerent again.

'He's on a course...'

'Yeah, right.' Justin clearly didn't believe her.

'A course to do with illnesses like Gemma's, as a matter of fact.'

'More like a golf course,' said Justin, then laughed at his own joke, laughter that, surprisingly, Gaby joined in with.

'That was good, that, Justin,' she said. 'A golf course. I like it!'

As Sandie and Omar moved away the pair of them were still chortling, together with Gemma who toddled over to investigate and climbed onto her father's knee.

'Thanks for that,' said Sandie, throwing Omar a grateful, sidelong glance. 'For one dreadful moment I thought he was going to punch one or both of us on the nose.'

'I know,' Omar admitted. 'So did I. Is there any history of violence there?'

'Not as far as we know.' Sandie shook her head. 'Plenty of verbal spats between the two of them but that seems to be as far as it goes. One thing I must say, though, is that they each in their own way seem devoted to Gemma.'

'And that, of course, is our main concern.' Omar paused and looked around the ward. 'Now, is there anyone else you want me to see?'

'Well,' Sandie replied, 'I haven't had a chance to see Lewis yet.'

'In that case I'll go and have a little chat with him,' said Omar. As he headed off in the direction of Lewis's bed Sandie made her way back to the office where Penny greeted her with raised eyebrows.

'I see your knight in shining armour leapt to your defence,' she said.

'What do you mean?' Sandie frowned.

'Just now when Justin Woods was cutting up rough. I've never seen anyone move so fast. Omar was down that ward to your rescue like greased lightning.'

'Don't be silly,' protested Sandie.

'Well, he *was*,' said Penny with a little shrug. 'I should watch him if I were you.'

'I don't know what you mean,' said Sandie. She felt embarrassed now, especially as Emma had heard Penny's remarks and looked as if she might be about to side with her. 'He would have done the same for anyone.'

'Well, let's hope so,' said Penny dryly. 'I don't know—supper last night, leaping to your rescue today. What next? I ask myself.'

'What's all this?' Emma's eyes widened as she looked at Sandie. 'Did he take you out to supper?'

'No,' Sandie replied quickly, 'no, of course he didn't.'

'It was the next best thing,' remarked Penny. When Sandie remained tight-lipped and Emma clearly wasn't going to let the matter drop, she said, 'He cooked supper for her. Isn't that right, Sandie?'

'He *what*?' squeaked Emma.

'Cooked supper for her,' Penny repeated.

'It wasn't quite how that sounds,' protested Sandie. 'He happens to live in the same place as I do and he did it as a welcome-home gesture because I've been away, that's all.'

'Right,' said Emma.

'He *did*,' said Sandie. Seeing that Emma clearly still didn't believe her, she sighed and moved away down the ward, carefully avoiding eye contact with Omar, who was sitting beside Lewis.

The nursing staff had just admitted a baby who had been repeatedly vomiting up his feeds and Penny had asked Sandie to examine him.

His parents, Claudia and Jack Maynard, who both looked frantic with worry, accompanied the baby, William.

'Hello,' said Sandie, smiling at both adults then down at William who was lying in his mother's arms, gazing up at a brightly coloured mobile of tiny yellow canaries and lovebirds. 'Mr and Mrs Maynard?' she said. When both adults nodded she added, 'And this must be William. I'm Dr Rawlings and I've come to examine William and to ask you a few questions.' She paused and as the baby's parents waited expectantly she went on, 'Now, I understand William is having problems with his feeding—is that right?'

'Yes, Doctor.' Claudia nodded and glanced at her husband.

'Can you tell me exactly what happens?' asked Sandie drawing up a chair and sitting in front of them.

'Well, he was feeding very well to start with,' said Claudia, 'then he started bringing up his milk.'

'Was this small quantities?' asked Sandie.

'At first.' Claudia nodded. 'But lately he's been bringing back the whole feed.'

'And does this just trickle out?'

'No.' It was Jack who answered now. 'More often than not he chucks it right across the room.'

'I see,' Sandie nodded. 'So what did you do about this?'

'I told the health visitor first,' Claudia replied. 'She said I should see my GP—that's Dr Meadows. He referred us here to Dr Forrester who said he wanted William admitted for tests and monitoring.'

'He said William may have a condition which affects a valve in his stomach,' Jack added.

Sandie nodded. 'Yes,' she said, 'that's right—it's a condition called pyloric stenosis.'

'It sounds awful,' said Claudia, her eyes filling with sudden tears.

'It can easily be put right,' Sandie hastened to assure her. 'Now, I see from your notes that William is your first baby.'

Claudia nodded, clearly overcome with emotion. 'We were late starters,' said Jack with a shy grin. 'We thought we couldn't have children for a long time then this little miracle came along.'

'And…now…now this…' choked Claudia.

'You mustn't upset yourself,' said Sandie gently. 'We have a first-class paediatric team here at Ellie's and I can assure you that William will have the best possible attention. You'll soon have him home again as right as rain. Now, I'd like to have a little look at him if I may. Could you just slip off his babysuit?'

While Claudia removed the baby's all-in-one suit and his vest, Sandie carefully warmed the head of her stethoscope. Then, while Claudia held the baby, she listened first to his back then his chest. 'No problems there,' she said as Claudia anxiously watched her face. 'Now, if you could just slip off his nappy— that's right.'

Moments later Claudia was dressing her son once more and Sandie was writing up his notes. 'Are you able to stay with William?' she asked as she finished and put her pen back in her top pocket. Out of the corner of her eye she saw Omar stand up and leave Lewis's bedside.

'Yes.' Claudia looked up and nodded. 'Sister Wiseman said I could stay in the mothers' room. Jack has to go to work, but he's coming back later.'

'Dr Forrester will see William tomorrow,' Sandie explained, 'but for today we are just going to monitor his feeds, his urine and his motions. I suggest you try and relax as much as you can.'

'Thank you, Doctor,' said Claudia. 'You've been very kind...' She trailed off as Omar stopped at the foot of William's cot.

'Hello,' he said. 'Who do we have here?'

'This is William Maynard,' Sandie explained. 'He's query pyloric stenosis. He's Dr Forrester's patient and these are his parents.' She turned to Claudia and Jack. 'This is Dr Nahum, our paediatric registrar,' she explained.

After Omar had acknowledged the Maynards he and Sandie moved away from the cot. 'Any problems?' he asked quietly.

'No,' she replied. 'It all seems perfectly straightforward. The baby is apparently feeding normally but then suffers projectile vomiting and brings back the entire feed. The parents understandably are very concerned. This is their first child and from what they told me they waited a long time for him.' She paused, suddenly very aware of Omar again and at the same time angry that she was. What on earth was the matter with her? Anyone would think she was some raw little student nurse on her first day on the wards, completely overwhelmed by the fact that some good-looking doctor had noticed her, when, in actual fact, she was a senior house officer with a long-term partner, thus putting herself firmly out of the dating arena. 'Tell me,' she said in a superhuman effort to pull herself together, 'how did you find Lewis?'

'You were quite right,' he replied smoothly, apparently oblivious to her inner turmoil. But why should he be otherwise? Unless, of course, he was only too aware of the effect he was having on her, a thought which made the whole thing seem suddenly unbearable. 'He is very lethargic and I fear he may be suffering new side effects from his chemotherapy. I am going to ask the oncologist to come and have a look at him.'

'Looks like his mother has just arrived,' said Sandie, as a tall, blonde-haired young woman came through the double doors to the ward.

'I'm sure she will want to speak to one of us,' said Omar.

'Shall I do it?' asked Sandie, as he glanced at his watch.

'Thank you, yes, if you would,' he replied. 'I have to go down to Special Care to see baby Augustus.'

'Are there problems with him?' asked Sandie quickly.

'Yes, I'm afraid so,' Omar replied. 'He's not responding as well as we'd hoped.'

He went then, leaving Sandie to cope with Karen Winter while he went off not only to see baby Augustus but also, no doubt, to placate Suki and Leroy Collingwood.

And so for Sandie and the rest of the staff on Paediatrics the relentless daily ward routine went on until, at last, she found a spare moment to grab a sandwich and a can of orange juice, which she took out into the hospital grounds. She found a garden seat with a plaque which stated that it had been donated by the Eleanor James Hospital League of Friends and which looked out across the large expanse of mossy grass at the front of the building where the branches of huge macrocarpa trees spread shade over almost the entire area.

With a sigh she sank down onto the seat, kicked off her shoes and lifted her face to the warmth of the sun. It was a relief to take a break from the relentless demands of the ward even though there was no guarantee that her pager wouldn't go off before she had a chance to take even a bite of her sandwich. She was on a twelve-hour shift that day and she knew she would need something to eat if she was to get through. It was also something of a relief to get away from Omar and the situation that seemed to be developing between them. What that situation was exactly Sandie wasn't entirely sure—she only knew that there was some aspect of her relationship with the registrar that she was beginning to find disturbing.

If asked, she would have been hard-pressed to say why she should find it disturbing, though it was something to do with that intense feeling of awareness she had whenever he was around. She couldn't even say he was objectionable or disagreeable in any way because he wasn't. There was nothing about Omar that could be classed as disagreeable. So what was it? she asked herself as she opened her packet of sandwiches and bit into one of them. Why should she be so aware of him? After all, it surely couldn't be that she was attracted to him. She had Jon, for heaven's sake. What more did she want? And Omar himself had Amanda so, no, it couldn't possibly be that... But just supposing she didn't have Jon, and supposing Omar didn't have Amanda? Would she be attracted to him then?

The answer, to her complete and utter consternation, came back loud and clear as a resounding yes. If she were free, yes, she would find Omar attractive. Who wouldn't? He was, after all, an incredibly attractive man and Sandie doubted there would be many women who wouldn't be smitten by those smouldering good looks and that easy, old-fashioned charm, almost boyish in its simplicity but with devastatingly sexy undertones that would be almost impossible to resist. And if he were free, would he find her attractive? He had hinted that he would but what did that mean exactly?

'Mind if I join you?'

Sandie looked up sharply to find a dark silhouette obscuring the sun. The features were in shadow but there was no mistaking the voice. 'Oh, no,' she said. 'No, of course not.' But because she had been thinking about him and because of the nature of those thoughts she was thrown into sudden turmoil, knocking over her can of orange juice and upsetting her sandwiches.

'Here,' he said, bending down and retrieving the can while she scrabbled for the sandwiches, 'let me help you. Sorry, I startled you…'

'No, no,' she said quickly, 'it's all right.' Thank goodness he didn't—couldn't—know what she had been thinking only seconds ago.

'I saw you out here,' he said. Glancing over his shoulder at the building behind, he went on, 'I was in the special care unit and I decided I needed a break and thought I would join you. I hope you don't mind.'

'No,' she said, hoping he couldn't hear the sudden hammering of her heart, 'no, of course not.'

'Some people like to be alone,' he said. 'They cherish those moments of solitude in the midst of a hectic day.'

'Well, it certainly gets . hectic,' agreed Sandie, as she struggled to regain her composure. 'I like to come out here for a while. It's so peaceful,' she added. 'Those trees are so majestic somehow...' She trailed off, terrified she was babbling. But she needn't have worried for he leaned back on the seat and put one arm along the back just the way he had the night before when he had sat on her sofa.

'I love those trees,' he said simply. 'They remind me of trees from my childhood in Somalia.'

'You actually lived in Somalia?' Sandie turned to him in surprise.

'For a time, yes.' He nodded. 'My father came from a village near Mogadishu—in fact, I still return there whenever I have the chance.'

'And your mother?'

'My mother was English. They are both dead now. They were killed in an uprising in Africa when I was seven years old.'

She stared at him in consternation. 'Oh,' she said. 'I'm sorry—I had no idea.'

'It's all right.' He gave a little shrug. 'It was a long time ago.'

'Even so, it must have been terrible for you at the time.'

'Yes,' he said quietly. 'Yes, it was.'

'So what happened to you? Where did you live?'

'My grandparents—my mother's parents—wanted me to come to England and live with them, but my father's family wanted me to stay with them.'

'So how was it decided?' Suddenly she was intensely interested in what had happened to this seven-year-old boy who had been so cruelly orphaned.

'My parents had left precise instructions in their wills that if anything should happen to them I should come to England. Luckily my Somali family recognised that it would be in my best interests to come here to be educated. Somalia is a very poor country,' he explained. 'There have been years of civil unrest followed by famine, and they knew I would have a better chance in this country.'

'How did your parents meet?' asked Sandie curiously.

'My father came to this country on a scheme sponsored by a charity and trained to be a doctor. He and my mother met at medical school. They married soon after they qualified. I was born here but when I was two they took me out to Africa where they were working for an aid agency. We were there until the incident in which they were killed.'

'Were you involved in the incident?'

'No.' Omar shook his head. 'They were travelling in the north of the country when they got caught up in an ambush—the whole region was run by warring warlords with no proper law and order. I was with my aunt who looked after me while my parents were away. On this occasion I believe they were taking medical supplies to the people of some of the far-flung villages and to the nomads who roam the plains of northern Somalia.'

Sandie frowned, trying to imagine what he was describing and failing miserably. 'It must have been terribly hard for you, coming back to England alone,' she said at last.

'Yes, I suppose it was.'

'You must have missed your Somali family after being with them for five years.'

'Yes, I did,' he said, and Sandie noticed that a far-away look had come into his eyes as if he was once again seeing the arid plains and villages of his childhood. Not for the first time she was aware of the proud, almost noble set of his head. 'Especially my aunt, Mitzi,' he went on. 'I was very fond of her, probably because she was the one who cared for me on a day-to-day basis.'

'Do you still see her when you return?'

'Oh yes.' A smile touched his features. 'I wouldn't dare miss her, and she is always overjoyed to see her nephew-boy—as she still calls me.'

'What about your English grandparents? Did you get on well with them?'

'Yes…' He hesitated as if unsure how much he should divulge, then, apparently coming to a decision, he said, 'I owe them everything. It can't have been easy for them, especially in the beginning. They had been opposed to my parents' marriage—they didn't approve of mixed marriages, as they called them, neither were they too happy when my father took their daughter off to that wild place. But when the test came they came through and have been there for me ever since. They paid for my education and financed me through medical school. And just to show how far we've come, they even came with me on a trip to Somalia a few years ago. The moment that they and Mitzi met is one I shall remember for the rest of my life.'

'They are still alive?'

'Yes, very much so, although they are both rather frail these days,' he replied. 'They live near Oxford and I get up to see them as often as I can. Maybe you will meet them one day, Sandie.'

'I should like that,' said Sandie, and she meant it, even if at the same time she realised that it was highly unlikely that there would be an occasion where she would meet his grandparents. 'I would also like to hear more about Somalia,' she said. 'It sounds a truly fascinating place.'

'It is,' he agreed. 'It is a place of such contrasts, such extremes—huge mountain ranges and plains in the north, bush country further south and the most glorious beaches and sand dunes on the Indian ocean coast.'

'It sounds wonderful,' she said dreamily.

'It is,' he agreed. 'It's also very hot. The temperature regularly reaches 120 degrees in the south but in the north, in the mountains, it can plunge to below freezing.'

'Do you ever want to go back there—to live, I mean, not just on holiday?'

'Yes,' he replied, 'I do, eventually. One day I will return to Africa to use my knowledge to help those people who are worse off than anything we can even begin to imagine in this country.' He paused as if considering just how much he should say. 'Do you know,' he said at last, as if rapidly reaching a decision, 'that less than a third of all the people in Somalia have access to clean drinking water?'

'No.' She shook her head. 'I didn't know. That's appalling and it's something we in the West so take for granted.' She hesitated. 'I thought about going to work for one of the aid organisations once. I saw a film about starving children in Ethiopia and I almost signed up to go.'

'What stopped you?' Omar turned his head to look at her.

'I don't know. I think it was at a crucial time career-wise for me and I decided it wasn't practical...'

'But you didn't rule it out completely?'

'No,' she agreed, 'not completely. I get so moved...so upset by these situations and yet at the same time I feel that what we are able to do is so small, so insignificant...a mere drop in the ocean.'

'No, Sandie,' he interrupted her. Taking her hand, he gazed urgently into her face. 'Don't ever think that. Every contribution, every offer of help makes a tremendous difference.'

She stared at him for a long moment, noting the passion in his eyes as he spoke, then suddenly he released her hand and his shoulders slumped a little. 'Sorry,' he said. 'I sound like one of those charity appeals on the radio—I didn't mean to.'

'It's all right,' she said gently. 'It's obviously something you feel very strongly about—and rightly so. Especially where you are so closely involved—' She broke off as his pager sounded.

'I'd better go,' he said, and he sounded reluctant, as if he'd have liked nothing better than to go on sitting there with her, talking about his beloved Somalia.

She glanced at her watch. 'I'll be in soon,' she said.

'Finish your drink,' he said. 'I'll leave you in peace now.'

She watched him walk away and found herself wondering anew about him. His talk of his background had both fascinated and surprised her. She had known about his close links with Somalia but she hadn't known that he had actually lived there as a child. The story of his

parents had been both romantic and heartbreaking: how they had met and married in the
face of parental opposition; how they had pursued a dream to help those less fortunate than
themselves and had lost their own lives in the
process. She wondered about his relatives, the
English grandparents who had raised and educated him, and his aunt in Africa who had
cared for him as a small boy and who still
loved him. It was a story that had touched her
deeply and fired her imagination, and at the
same time it was a story about which she
wanted to know more. She had been intrigued
by Omar's talk of Africa, a continent which
had always held a fascination for her, and she
had almost felt the essence of Somalia when
he had been talking—the heat, the arid, unpre-
dictable terrain and its proud, nomadic people.
Maybe in time he would tell her more.

She glanced at her watch and with a little
sigh rose to her feet. It was high time she was
back on the ward. Almost with a sense of reluctance she left the garden, the majestic macrocarpas and the memories they had evoked

for Omar, and made her way back into the hospital.

She didn't see Omar again that day for on returning to the ward it was to find that he had been called urgently to the special care baby unit where yet another newborn premature baby was fighting for its life. When at last her shift was over and she thankfully made her way to the car park there was still no sign of him, neither was his car in the space reserved for him. No doubt, she thought ruefully, his shift had ended hours ago and he was already at home. Were shorter hours one of the perks reserved for registrars? With a wry little smile she drove past the macrocarpas and down the beech-lined avenue to the main road.

When she reached Pitt's Place it was to find Omar's car already on the forecourt and she knew her assumption had been correct. It was very quiet in the large old house, just faint sounds coming from some of the other apartments—the signature tune of a well-known television soap opera, voices, a snatch of music—but that was all, and from Omar's apartment not a sound.

The first thing she did after checking the mail, which always arrived long after she'd left for work in the mornings, was to take a shower then think about what she would cook for her evening meal. Last night Omar had arrived with food—had it really only been last night? It seemed much longer ago than that. In fact, it seemed as if she had known him forever. But it was highly unlikely that would happen again tonight. She smiled to herself when she recalled she had been annoyed the previous evening and found herself thinking that if it happened now she would be quite pleased, especially in view of how tired she was. Even as the thought crossed her mind her doorbell sounded, and with a smile she hurried to the door and opened it, fully expecting to see Omar there and feeling decidedly disappointed to find Julie instead. In that fleeting moment the irony of the situation hit her. The previous evening she had expected Julie and it had been Omar, and tonight she had hoped—yes, hoped—that it would be Omar, and it was Julie.

'Sandie?' She was suddenly aware that Julie was peering at her. 'Are you all right?'

'Oh, yes. Yes, I'm fine.'

'You looked surprised to see me.'

'Er, yes, I was a bit.'

'You did say come for a drink when I saw you this morning. Had you forgotten?'

'No of course not.' She *had* forgotten but didn't want to admit as much to Julie. 'Come in,' she said. 'I'll get you a glass of wine.'

'Maybe you thought it was Omar again,' said Julie, coming right into the apartment and shutting the door behind her.

'Omar?' said Sandie over her shoulder as she headed for the kitchen. 'Heavens, no, why on earth should I think that?'

'Well, after last night's little episode,' said Julie, following her into the kitchen.

'That was a one-off,' Sandie replied firmly, taking a bottle of white wine from the fridge, 'and not something I'm expecting to be re-peated.'

'Just as well,' said Julie with a little shrug, 'especially as he's got Amanda in there with him tonight.'

CHAPTER FIVE

IT THREW Sandie, so much so that she found herself wishing that Julie would go, which wasn't like her at all for usually she liked it when Julie or Rob popped in for a drink and a chat. But this time as she and Julie talked, an image of Omar and Amanda hovered somewhere around the edges of her thoughts, an image that became more disturbing by the minute as inevitably she found herself wondering what they were doing. Not, of course, that it was any business of hers who Omar invited to his apartment or what he did. It was just that briefly, that afternoon, as they had sat together in the shade of the trees and he had told her about his life, she had felt incredibly close to him, so much so that she was eager, almost desperate to know more. But surely she hadn't expected him to come to her apartment again that evening? Had she? No, of course she hadn't, she told herself firmly as with only half an ear she listened to Julie going on and

118

on about her latest boyfriend. But although she might not have expected him, had she secretly been hoping that he would come?

Of course not.

But hadn't she been disappointed when she'd opened the door and found Julie there? She couldn't deny it, any more than she could deny the fact that she was miserable now she'd found that Amanda was with him in his apartment.

'So, what do you think?'

'I'm sorry?' Sandie stared at Julie, realising to her horror that her friend had been talking to her and she hadn't heard a word she'd been saying because her thoughts had all been on Omar.

'I said, what do you think I should do?' Julie paused and peered at Sandie from beneath her thick fringe of hair. 'You weren't listening, were you?' she said accusingly. 'You were miles away.'

'I'm sorry, Julie, really I am,' Sandie said quickly. 'I've got rather a lot on my mind at the moment, that's all. Now, tell me again, what is it you wanted to know?'

'I was just talking about Guy.' Julie gave a little sniff and Sandie felt guilty that her friend might have thought she simply wasn't interested in her or her problems.

'So how is he?' Julie had been seeing Guy Sinclair, who was a registrar on Orthopaedics, since well before Sandie had gone to Manchester.

'He's OK.' Julie shrugged. 'Very well, in fact.'

'So what's the problem?' Sandie forced herself to concentrate.

'It's just that he doesn't seem to have heard of the word ''commitment'',' Julie replied.

'It wasn't so long ago that commitment was the last thing on your mind,' observed Sandie. 'I can well remember you telling me that you felt you had it all—good job, lovely home, friends and the occasional relationship.'

'Yes,' Julie admitted, 'I know…'

'Well, what's changed?'

'I'm not sure,' said Julie slowly, 'I guess… Oh, I don't know.'

'I can tell you exactly what's changed,' Sandie said firmly. Julie threw her a startled glance, and she went on, 'It's Guy—that's what's changed. You didn't really care much about any of the others so you weren't too bothered about any sort of long-term commitment. With Guy it's different. I would say quite simply that you are in love with Guy and you want to be able to plan a future with him.'

'You think so?' Julie stared at her.

'Yes, I do.' Sandie nodded. 'What you have to do now is to bring Guy round to your way of thinking.'

'And that could be easier said than done. Any talk of engagements, weddings or babies and his eyes seem to glaze over.'

'Are you bringing him to Kate's wedding?'

'Oh, yes. He wasn't keen at first but I wouldn't take any excuses,' replied Julie.

'Well, that's a start anyway.' Sandie laughed.

'Do you have this problem with Jon?' asked Julie curiously as Sandie leaned forward and topped up her glass. 'You've been going out together for a long time now, haven't you? Is he reluctant when it comes to commitment?'

'Not really.' Sandie shrugged but for some reason at the mention of Jon she felt a pang deep inside that she couldn't identify. 'We've always been together and it's a foregone conclusion that one day we will get married...and have a family.'

'Is he coming down for the wedding?'

'Yes, but I don't know how long he'll be able to stay.'

'Well, who knows?' Julie gave a deep sigh. 'Maybe the wedding will work wonders and we could both end up with diamonds on our left hands.'

'Yes, maybe.' Sandie joined in Julie's laughter but strangely the thought of that—of her and Jon actually announcing their engagement to their families and friends, of buying and showing off a ring—left her feeling cold and empty. Surely she shouldn't feel that way? Surely if Jon did finally get around to a proper proposal and they started to make plans for their wedding, she would feel on top of the world? Maybe if and when it actually happened she would feel differently, she told herself as at last Julie stood up and announced that she needed to get back to her apartment.

Almost with a sense of relief Sandie walked to the door with Julie, bade her friend goodnight then watched as she walked along the corridor to the main first-floor landing and her own apartment. After Julie had turned the corner and was out of sight, Sandie turned and glanced the other way to the end of the corridor, towards Omar's apartment. The door was tightly shut and once again she found herself wondering what was taking place behind that door. Were Omar and Amanda talking, was he telling her about his childhood in Africa just the way he had told *her* earlier that day? Was he describing the place to her, telling her of the visits he had made there since? Had he told her about his grandparents and his Aunt Mitzi?

Somehow she doubted it, although she wasn't entirely sure why she doubted it. It was just that it seemed far more likely that he had cooked a meal for Amanda, had opened a bottle of wine over which they had lingered, maybe opened a second before…before… Why, even at this very moment they were probably making love.

The thought disturbed her more than she was prepared to admit, even to herself, and with a sharp little intake of breath she drew back into her apartment and shut her door with a loud snap. She hadn't seen inside Omar's apartment but somehow she imagined it would be opulent, with rich fabrics and loud paintings, no doubt symbolising the Somali side of his background and culture.

And what of Amanda herself? With her rather flamboyant style, her vibrant looks and flaming red hair, was she the type of woman that appealed to Omar?

Walking back into her apartment, Sandie stared at her reflection in the mirror above her mantelpiece. Maybe her own slightly olive skin, dark hair and green eyes simply left him cold. But what if they did? What did it matter? What possible consequences could there be, whether he did or did not find her attractive? And why should it matter to her whether or not he and Amanda were innocently talking about their past lives or whether they were engaged in the most torrid sex?

Nothing, she told herself firmly as she turned miserably away from the mirror. Nothing at all. So, if that was the case, why was it that an image of the pair of them engaged in the most erotic of situations continued to haunt her not only for the rest of the evening but also for long after she had gone to bed, where she lay for what seemed like hours, staring at the ceiling and imagining she heard sounds from that other apartment— which was impossible, given the fact that Omar's apartment was on the opposite side of the corridor—sounds of love-making, sighs, moans and cries of delight.

At last, totally unable to sleep and in steadily mounting frustration, she sat up, switched on her bedroom light and decided to phone Jon, hoping that he wouldn't already have gone to bed. His mobile phone was switched off, however, and his voicemail announcement invited her to leave a message. With a sigh she replaced the receiver. Maybe he was on duty…or perhaps he was out.

At last she slept, but it was a fitful sleep with vivid dreams: dreams of mountains and vast plains; of camel trains; of two people arguing violently, two people who started as Gemma's parents, Justin and Gaby, and finished as Omar Nahum and Amanda Cromer.

'Lewis is to go for a scan.' It was the following morning and Penny was just passing on a directive from the oncologist.

'Is he still lethargic?' asked Sandie.

'He's not right,' Penny answered. 'I only hope they can find out what the trouble is and treat him accordingly. He's been such a brave little chap throughout all his treatment, we were all hoping we'd seen the last of it.'

'I'll go and have a chat with him,' said Sandie. 'Is his mother in yet this morning?'

'No, she phoned in to say she's going to the school first—her daughter Lucy is in a school concert.'

Moving down the ward, Sandie stopped at the foot of Lewis's bed. The little boy was lying very still with the brim of his cap pulled down over his eyes. 'Hello, Lewis,' she said. She spoke softly, thinking that if he was asleep she wouldn't disturb him. She was on the point of moving quietly away when he spoke.

'I'm not asleep,' he said gruffly.

'Oh, that's good,' Sandie replied. 'I was looking forward to having a chat with you but I didn't want to wake you up if you were asleep. How are you feeling this morning?' she asked, drawing up a chair and sitting beside the bed.

'All right,' he said.

'No more being sick?'

'No.' He fell silent again and Sandie was just on the point of asking him about a video she saw on his locker when he spoke again. 'Guess what?' he said, pushing back his cap.

'You tell me,' she said.

'I've got to have another scan.'

'Really?' Sandie feigned surprise, letting him impart this piece of news.

'Yes.' He nodded. 'Today.'

'I see,' said Sandie. 'Well, you've had them before, haven't you? So at least you know all about them.'

'They don't hurt,' he said.

'No,' Sandie agreed, 'they don't hurt. Is your mum coming in later?'

'Yes, she'll come with me for the scan. She's gone to Lucy's school concert first.'

'Lucy is your sister?'

'Yes, she's eight,' Lewis replied. Raising himself onto his elbows, he looked across at Sam Wallis's bed. 'He cried in the night,' he said.

'I expect he was missing his mum,' said Sandie.

Lewis nodded. 'I miss my mum too, but I've got used to it now.'

'You've been going into hospitals for a long time now, haven't you, Lewis?'

'Since I was five,' he said solemnly, 'and I'm nearly seven now.'

'Well, let's hope you'll soon be able to go home with your family again. Now, what are you going to do until it's time for your scan?'

'Don't know.'

'I know,' said Sandie. 'How about I move the television and video over here? Then, if you were to watch your video, maybe Sam would watch it as well. It might help to cheer him up. What do you think?'

'All right,' said Lewis, reaching up onto his locker for the video.

Five minutes later Sandie left Lewis deeply engrossed in the Disney adventure and to her satisfaction she saw that Sam had lowered the bedcovers and shown some interest in what was happening on the screen.

'They both seem happy for the moment,' Sandie reported to Penny.

'Oh, well done,' Penny replied, looking down the ward to the corner that housed the two boys. 'We haven't had any luck at all with getting Sam interested in anything and Lewis, well, poor little boy…' She trailed off but what she left unsaid was somehow a hundred times more poignant than what she had expressed, and simply reflected the collective anxiety of the staff for this small but so brave patient.

The next hour for Sandie was spent in writing up reports and medication charts. Almost before she knew it, the consultants had arrived on the ward for their morning round and, of course, Omar was with them. After the disturbed night she had spent, Sandie had decided that in future she would not let herself be affected by Omar or by anything he might say or do. She had finally convinced herself that the thoughts and feelings she had been experiencing where he was concerned were completely and utterly ridiculous and would quite simply have to stop. And if that meant that Omar himself had to be discouraged then that was what had to happen.

With this resolve now uppermost in her mind, Sandie stood up, smoothed down her white coat and stepped out of Penny's office to join the ward round.

Her decision lasted precisely two minutes and then Omar's eyes met hers, he smiled at her and her heart turned over. Spontaneously she smiled back and it was only then that she remembered her resolve of earlier, together with the recollection of what had presumably taken place in his apartment the night before. Quickly she lowered her gaze.

Matt had obviously had time to study Gemma's test results for he had drawn up a treatment plan for the little girl, which involved a drug regime in conjunction with a strictly controlled diet.

'So how long will this go on for?' demanded Justin when Matt explained the situation.

'For as long as it takes to make her better,' Matt replied patiently. 'We will have her in from time to time to review her condition.'

'So she won't have to stay on all this for ever then?' Gaby stared up at the ring of faces around Gemma's bed where the little girl was happily playing with Omar's stethoscope.

'Hopefully, no,' Matt replied, 'but I have to emphasise that her diet will be crucial.' He paused and Sandie guessed that he was wondering how Gaby would cope with such a situation. 'Do you have anyone who will help you with Gemma's diet?' he said at last.

'Me mum will,' said Gaby, ignoring Justin.

'And when she's wiv me, me girlfriend will,' said Justin.

'I don't want her touching Gemma.' Gaby rounded on him.

Pre-empting another spat, Sandie swiftly intervened. 'We'll talk about it later,' she said, her voice both firm and soothing.

The consultants moved on and the ward round continued. It was decided that baby William would have surgery on the following day to correct his pyloric stenosis and it was left to Sandie and Emma to placate and calm his agitated mother. By the time the group reached Lewis's and Sam's corner, the two boys were transfixed by the antics of the cartoon characters on the screen.

Penny gave Sam's progress report to the orthopaedic surgeon who studied it carefully. 'He's doing well,' he said.

'Do you want to examine him?' asked Penny.

'I don't think so.' The surgeon shook his head. 'It would be a shame to disturb him.'

'That's certainly the happiest we've seen him since his accident,' Penny replied.

As Penny spoke, Lewis looked round and Sandie knew he had heard the sister's remark. The group moved on and she bent down and very quietly, so that only Lewis himself could hear, she said, 'Well done, Lewis—I knew you'd be the one to cheer Sam up.'

The little boy grinned up at her from beneath his cap and gave a thumbs-up sign.

Sandie hurried to catch the rest of the group up and felt Omar's eyes on her again, but this time she was ready for it, this time she ignored it, and even afterwards, when the consultants left the ward and Omar lingered, she refused to grant him eye contact.

Somehow, throughout the rest of the week Sandie managed to maintain her coolness towards the new paediatric registrar, instinct telling her that this was the only way she could deal with the awareness of him that had crept up on her in such a disturbing manner. As far as Omar himself was concerned, Sandie knew he was puzzled by this new coolness on her part for on occasion he would catch her unawares as she went about her duties, and she would look up and see bewilderment in those dark eyes. If she was honest, it hurt her to see it, but every instinct warned her that it could be dangerous to let her friendship with this man develop. After the anguish she'd suffered that night when she had imagined him and Amanda together, she knew in her heart that friendship with Omar could very quickly deepen into something else. And she couldn't let that happen. She had Jon, and Jon himself would be arriving very soon for Kate's and Tom's wedding.

On the ward, baby William had his operation and recovered very quickly to the delight of his parents. A child was admitted for investigation with severe allergies ranging from eczema, which covered eighty per cent of her body, to asthma and food allergies. Sam continued to make slow but steady progress, but the results of Lewis's scan were worrying, with new evidence of the neuroblastoma having spread to his lymph glands, resulting in a plan for yet more treatment.

'He seems to take it all in his stride,' said Penny as she and Sandie observed the little boy, 'and he's been brilliant with Sam. Mr Jefferson has said he can go home for a couple of days before we start the new treatment.'

'He'll like that,' said Sandie, 'but Sam will miss him.'

On the special care unit baby Augustus continued to battle for life and two more very premature babies were born, both of whom needed to be put onto ventilators to enable them to breathe.

'Are you all ready for this wedding?' asked Penny as at last on Friday evening Sandie completed her final ward round and entered up the last of her notes.

'I think so, just about.' Sandie nodded wearily. She'd been hoping to get away earlier but there had been one delay after another.

'Is Jon coming down tonight?'

She shook her head. 'No, he'd been hoping to but he can't get away. He's on duty until ten o'clock so he's driving down first thing in the morning. It's a good job the wedding isn't until three, so he should be here in plenty of time.'

'Will he be able to stay the whole weekend?'

'I hope so. With a bit of luck he will drive back on Sunday night.'

'What are you wearing?' asked Penny.

'I have a long, crêpe dress in a sort of biscuit colour—oh, and a straw hat.'

'That'll look lovely with your dark colouring,' said Penny, then wistfully added, 'And you're so slim as well.'

'What about you, what are you wearing?' Sandie stood up from the desk and gave a little stretch.

'A two-piece,' Penny replied, 'matching dress and jacket—sort of a dusky pink. I bought it for our Ben's graduation.'

'Nice.' Sandie nodded. 'Wonder what Kate will wear.'

'Don't know—it's a secret apparently. This is the first wedding I've been to that hasn't taken place either in church or a register office.'

'And me,' Sandie replied. 'It'll certainly be different but Gainsborough Hall is the most wonderful setting for a wedding.'

'Well, I'm looking forward to it,' Penny declared. 'It's about time we had another wedding around here. We haven't had one for ages. And I think it's wonderful that Kate and Tom have found happiness together.'

The south of England had been enjoying an Indian summer—days filled with warmth and sunshine, with the rich hues of the leaves providing a perfect foil for the deep cobalt blue of the skies. The morning of Kate's and Tom's wedding was no exception and dawned fair and bright with more than a promise of warmth to come. At Pitt's Place a light mist hung over the dew-soaked lawns, shrouding the last of the summer roses, and even before it had completely cleared Jon roared up the drive in his sports car. Sandie, watching his arrival from the landing window, knew a moment's sense of relief. Dear Jon, with his wide, open smile, fresh complexion and fair hair that flopped over his forehead and which he was forever pushing back, was just what she needed, especially now when she had been experiencing these disquieting thoughts over Omar. Jon, with his down-to-earth, laid-back style, would put paid to all that once and for all.

Moments later, after running down the stairs, she opened the front door and was clasped in his arms. It felt good. Warm and safe, just as she'd known it would.

'Oh, Jon,' she sighed, lifting her face for his kiss. 'I'm so, so pleased you could come.'

'Hi, Sandie.' He hugged her tightly then released her, appearing faintly surprised by her enthusiasm.

'How was your journey?' she asked, following him as he returned to his car and retrieved the suit he obviously intended to wear to the wedding.

'Pretty good,' he replied. 'I was on the motorway before anyone else realised the sun was up.'

'Well, that's good,' she said. 'Anyway, come on up. I bet you're dying for a cup of tea.' Jon was a renowned tea-drinker and had never been known to refuse a cup.

'You can say that again.' He grinned and side by side they began climbing the wide staircase to the first-floor apartments. As they reached the top Omar suddenly appeared and walked across the landing to meet them. Sandie's heart sank. She had been hoping that she wouldn't have to introduce Jon to Omar until they were at the wedding when there would be a lot of other people around. Why she felt that way, she had no idea. She only knew she didn't want to make an issue of their meeting. Now, it appeared, she had no choice.

'Hello.' Omar smiled in his easy manner. 'You must be Jon. I've heard all about you.'

'Really?' Jon raised his eyebrows and as Omar held out his hand he gripped it in his own. Before Sandie had a chance to speak he said, 'And you must be Sandie's new neighbour, the one who cooks supper for her.'

'That was only once,' protested Sandie, as Omar laughed. 'But, yes, this is Omar Nahum, Jon. Omar is our paediatric registrar at Ellie's.'

'Oh, so he's on your department as well.' It was spoken innocently enough but to Sandie, who was feeling vulnerable anyway because of the thoughts she'd had concerning Omar, it seemed to hold a hint of accusation.

'Yes,' she said quickly, then half turning to Omar she went on rapidly, 'Omar, Jon's an SHO in Accident and Emergency.'

'Chester, isn't it?' asked Omar, as the two men stood back after shaking hands.

'That's right.'

'And you've just driven down this morning?' When Jon nodded Omar went on, 'Well, at least you can relax now for the rest of the weekend. Are you able to stay over till Monday or will it be a late Sunday night return?'

'Actually,' said Jon, throwing Sandie an uneasy glance, 'that's the bad news, I'm afraid. I haven't had a chance to tell Sandie yet, but I have to go back tonight straight after the wedding.'

'Oh, Jon!' Sandie stared at him in dismay. 'I knew you couldn't stay for long but I thought at least until tomorrow…'

'I'm sorry, Sandie,' he said, 'really I am, but we are so short-staffed at the moment, what with holidays and sickness—well, you know what it's like. I don't need to tell you.'

'Oh, well,' Sandie sighed, suddenly once again acutely aware of Omar as he stood silently by, not commenting in any way but taking in the facts of the scene unfolding before him. 'I suppose it can't be helped. At least you are here for the wedding—Kate and Tom will be pleased about that.'

'Talking of the wedding,' said Omar smoothly, 'I've ordered a cab. Would you two care to share it with me? I understand the parking at the hotel is rather limited.'

'Oh,' Sandie began, about to refuse, thinking that Jon wouldn't like that, that he would want to go either in her car or his own, 'that's very kind of you, but—'

'Thank you,' Jon intervened. 'That would be great.'

'Good.' Omar nodded. 'In that case, why don't the two of you join me in my apartment for a drink before we go? Shall we say two o'clock?'

'Yes, all right,' Sandie heard herself say.

'I'll see you later, then.' With a smile Omar continued on his way down the stairs, leaving Sandie to lead the way along the corridor to her apartment.

'I'm sorry, Sandie,' said Jon again as she shut the door behind them, 'about having to go back so soon, but it was either that or not come at all.'

'Well, it can't be helped,' she replied, 'and, as you say, it's better that than nothing. And it's not as if we haven't seen each other recently, is it?'

'No,' he agreed, 'it isn't.' After hanging his suit on the wardrobe door in the bedroom, he followed Sandie into the kitchen where she was filling the kettle. 'He seems a nice guy, your neighbour. What was his name again?'

'Omar,' she replied. 'Omar Nahum. Yes, he's OK.' She didn't want to talk about Omar. It was enough that they would have to spend time with him later without talking about him as well.

Jon, it seemed, had other ideas. 'Where did you say he's from?' he asked, leaning across the worktop and looking out of the window into the garden.

'Well, his mother was English, but his father was from Somalia. It's a sad but terribly romantic story,' Sandie went on. 'They met when they were at medical school and married against parental wishes then, after Omar was born, they returned to Africa to work. They were both killed in some sort of uprising and eventually Omar came back to this country to live with his grandparents.'

'You seem to know a lot about him,' observed Jon lightly.

'Not really.' In spite of herself, Sandie felt the colour touch her cheeks and she turned away quickly to hide it from Jon. 'It's only what I've learnt in passing, really.' Carefully she made the tea then, turning to Jon, she said, 'Come and give me a cuddle.'

Obediently he gathered her into his arms and once again she was happy to stay there a while, feeling the steady beating of his heart through the fabric of his shirt.

When at last they drew apart, again Sandie was aware of that feeling she'd had when she'd seen Jon while she'd been in Manchester, a feeling that there was a slight emotional distance between them, a feeling which, where Jon was concerned, she'd never before experienced.

'Jon?' she said, puzzled by this. 'Is everything all right?'

'Yes,' he said quickly—too quickly? 'Everything's fine. Why shouldn't it be?'

'I don't know, it's just that you seem a bit...I don't know, really. Are you tired?'

'Ah, well, if it's tiredness you're talking about then I guess we doctors have the monopoly on that,' he said with a rueful grin. 'In actual fact, Sandie, if you don't mind, I thought I might get my head down for a couple of hours before we get ready for the wedding...what with being on a late shift last night, driving down this morning then driving back again tonight for another shift tomorrow.'

'Of course I don't mind,' said Sandie quickly. 'You must get some rest.' To her surprise she found she meant it. In the past they would have made love, tired or not. At one time they would hardly have been able to wait, especially when they had been apart but now not only did Jon not seem so eager but Sandie also found she was actually rather relieved. Why that should be she wasn't really sure, neither did she feel she wanted to pursue the reasons—not today with a wedding to attend.

Later, after drinking the tea and eating toast, chatting amiably enough together about their respective families and mutual friends and discussing their work, Jon went for a rest while Sandie took a long, leisurely bath and washed her hair, then while her hair dried she gave herself a French manicure. When Jon woke up it was time for them both to get dressed for the wedding, Jon in the dark pinstriped suit, white shirt and silk tie he'd brought with him and Sandie in the dress she'd described to Penny. Her freshly washed hair touched her shoulders like a glossy curtain and apart from some gold jewellery her only adornment was two small red poppies fastened to the band of her straw hat.

'You look great,' said Jon when she was ready.

'You don't look so bad yourself,' she replied lightly.

'Ah, we medics scrub up pretty well when we have to.' Jon glanced at his watch. 'Isn't it time we went to your friend's for that drink?'

It was on the tip of Sandie's tongue to correct him, to say that Omar wasn't her friend, that he was no more than a neighbour and colleague, but something stopped her as she found herself unable to deny the fact. She may have only known Omar for a very short space of time and during that time she'd had many battles over her feelings towards him, but deep down and somewhat to her surprise she knew that she would never deny the fact Omar was her friend—even to Jon—at the same time she was well aware that it could be allowed to go no further than friendship.

CHAPTER SIX

SHE'D been wrong about Omar's apartment, Sandie thought as she sat on the edge of a black leather chesterfield and gazed around her. Far from the rich opulence she had expected, it appeared more minimalist than anything with plain walls, leather and glass furnishings and highly polished, stripped wooden floors. The only concession to ornament and the link to his culture, which Sandie had expected, was a wall-hanging of an African elephant above the fireplace. Omar himself had appeared in the doorway in response to their knock. He looked stunning in cream trousers and a black shirt, and as he took in her own appearance Sandie felt her pulse race.

'You look lovely, Sandie,' he said admiringly, and just in case his appreciation could be misinterpreted he turned to Jon. 'Doesn't she?' he added.

'She certainly does,' Jon replied. 'I can always count on Sandie to look gorgeous for any occasion. Trouble is, she usually ruins it by turning up late.' He gave a short laugh and Sandie held her breath, fully expecting Omar to say that she had been late the first time he'd met her, when he had been presiding over a staff meeting. But he remained silent, instead leading them into his apartment.

'I have champagne on ice,' he said, disappearing, presumably into the kitchen, after he had invited them both to sit down.

'This is nice,' said Sandie, looking around.

'You like it?' Jon frowned.

'Yes, I do.' She nodded slowly.

'Too plain for me,' Jon replied. 'I like a place to look like home—you know, books and magazines and things. This reminds me of the operating theatre…'

'Ssh,' said Sandie, 'he'll hear you.' Suddenly it became terribly important that Omar shouldn't hear any criticism either of himself or his lifestyle.

'Sandie tells me you're from Somalia,' said Jon as Omar came back into the room bearing glasses in one hand and an ice bucket with a bottle of champagne in the other.

Sandie threw Omar a quick glance, afraid now that he would think she'd been gossiping about him, and that was the last thing she wanted.

'My father's family are from Somalia,' Omar replied, setting the ice bucket down on a low table, its pedestal a gnarled, twisted piece of a tree trunk, its top a thick slab of smoked glass. 'I lived there briefly as a boy but most of my life has been spent in this country with my mother's family.' Bending over the table, he poured champagne into the flutes and just for a moment Sandie was reminded of that other occasion they had drank champagne together, when he had come to her flat.

'I think,' he said raising his glass, 'that today the toast must be to Tom and Kate.'

'Yes,' Sandie agreed. 'Tom and Kate.' She took a sip of her champagne. The sentiment was echoed by Jon who did likewise.

'Tell me about Tom,' Jon said, setting his glass down. 'I don't know him very well. Kate I have met on several occasions when I've been down but I don't know Tom.'

'He's divorced,' said Sandie, 'and he has two children. We were all delighted when he and Kate got together. Kate's husband was killed in a motorbike accident a couple of years ago. She also has two children,' she added, 'Siobhan and Connor.'

'I have been wondering who will be running Ellie's today,' said Omar with a wry smile. 'Everyone seems to be going to the wedding.'

'I know,' said Sandie with a laugh, 'Penny told me they are relying heavily on agency staff.'

They chatted on easily and comfortably and to Sandie's relief the slight tension she'd been aware of earlier between the two men seemed to dissolve, so much so that by the time the cab that Omar had booked arrived it was as if they'd known each other for years. At last Sandie herself relaxed and prepared to enjoy the afternoon.

Gainsborough Hall was a beautiful old house, built in the nineteenth century and set in acres of landscaped gardens and lush parkland. When the cab deposited Omar, Sandie and Jon at the imposing front entrance many other guests were also arriving, some in their own cars, others in taxis and some, from the hospital, in a large minibus.

Amanda, resplendent in a tight-fitting, emerald green silk suit that emphasised her voluptuous figure and mass of red hair emerged from a cab which drew in behind theirs. Omar immediately went back to her, paid her driver and greeted her with a kiss. Sandie found herself looking away.

'Who's that?' murmured Jon out of the side of his mouth.

'His current girlfriend,' Sandie replied in the same low tone.

'Hmm,' said Jon. 'Looks as if he could have his work cut out there.'

'Quiet,' whispered Sandie. 'He's bringing her over…'

'Jon,' said Omar, 'I'd like you to meet Amanda.' Turning to Amanda, who was eyeing Jon with interest, he said, 'Amanda, this is Jon… I'm sorry, I don't know your surname.'

'Markham,' Jon replied, taking Amanda's outstretched hand and dropping a kiss on it. 'Jon Markham.'

'Pleased to meet you,' said Amanda with a little laugh. 'So, what do you do, Jon Markham?'

'Jon is a doctor,' said Omar. 'He is also Sandie's boyfriend.'

Amanda half turned and glanced at Sandie, as if she had only just become aware of her presence. 'Really?' she said, her tone expressing surprise. It was as if she would never have put Sandie and this handsome doctor together in a million years, thought Sandie wryly.

'I think we should make our way inside,' said Omar. He was wearing his jacket now and the simplicity of the cream suit against his black shirt was drawing several admiring glances from various female guests as they climbed the steps and entered the hotel foyer. The marriage celebration was to take place in the hotel's orangery, an elegant building of pink brick with mullioned windows, which ran the entire width of the hotel. The guests were shown to their places in rows of velvet-covered chairs by Tom's son, Joe, and Kate's son, Connor, both looking grown up and handsome in suits. Sandie found herself seated between Jon and Omar. Amanda was on Omar's other side and Emma was seated beside Jon. In the row in front Penny, looking lovely in dusky pink, was seated with her husband Gavin. She turned round briefly and spoke to Sandie and greeted Jon whom she'd met before.

And then it seemed in no time at all the registrar was taking her place and the wedding party was arriving. Tom and Matt—the best man—arrived first, both men resplendent in morning dress, and took their places at the front of the assembled guests. After a suitable interval, amidst a little ripple of excited speculation and to the strains of a soft melody played by a pianist in one corner of the orangery, Kate herself arrived, looking cool and elegant in a champagne-coloured, 1920s-style dress and matching cloche hat and bearing oyster pink roses. Her daughter Siobhan and Tom's daughter Francesca accompanied her dressed in cream, ankle-length dresses trimmed with pink rosebuds and with pearls and roses in their hair.

As the assembled company rose to its feet Sandie felt the tears prickle at her eyelids. She always cried at weddings and it seemed this one was to be no exception. She'd thought she

might not this time, with it being quite uncon-
ventional and with both the bride and groom
being older and having been married before
and with children, but it made no difference.
That lump was there in her throat and by the
time Tom and Kate turned to face each other
and exchange the promises to love one another
for ever the tears were rolling steadily down
her cheeks.

It was Omar who saw them, Omar who quietly and without any fuss handed her a folded
white handkerchief. Gratefully she took it,
pressing it under her eyes so as not to smudge
her mascara. Lifting her head, her gaze met his
from beneath the brim of her straw hat and in
the intimacy of that special moment, as their
friends exchanged their vows, she was forced
to look quickly away, confused and alarmed
by what she saw in Omar's dark eyes.

The words of the promises affected Sandie
deeply but when she threw a sidelong glance
at Jon, hoping that he too might feel the same
way, it was to find that he appeared unmoved
by the ceremony. Throughout it all he didn't
as much as take her hand. Had she been wrong
all along in assuming that this was what he

wanted? Had it only been her who had assumed that their relationship would end in
marriage? And if it did, was it really what she
wanted? As the question entered her mind she
found for the first time she was unable to answer it. In the past she would have answered
unhesitatingly that Jon was the only man she
had ever wanted—so why not now? Suddenly
she felt a chill touch her spine and goose-
bumps appeared on her bare arms for with a
sudden flash of certainty she knew that the reason for her inability to answer her own question lay with the man who stood on her other
side, the man who a moment ago had shown
such concern for her tears.

But that was crazy, the voice of reason re-
monstrated. After all, she hardly knew this
man. Her friends had warned her he was a
heartbreaker and, if all that wasn't enough, he
was already in a relationship with someone
else.

So why, oh, why did she feel this way? Why
couldn't she simply enjoy the day and the fact
that Jon—the man she loved and hoped to
marry—was here beside her? Why had that
lump stuck in her throat as her friends had

pledged their lives to each other and why now was she feeling a moment of unutterable sadness?

When the ceremony was over, amidst a flurry of congratulations to the newlyweds, the assembled throng made its way from the orangery and into the hotel reception where drinks were being served. Now that the tension and emotion of the ceremony was over everyone relaxed, and there was much chatter and laughter. Many photographs were taken of the wedding group, not only by the official photographer but also by friends and relatives of Kate and Tom, until at last it was time to drift into the hotel dining room for the wedding reception.

The room with its glittering overhead chandeliers and marble pillars faced south, overlooking the hotel grounds and the sun terrace, while each of the white-clad round tables bore a centrepiece of pink roses and was set for eight guests. Sandie and Jon found themselves seated with Julie and her boyfriend, Guy, Penny and Gavin and another couple who turned out to be friends of Tom from his medical school days. Sandie wasn't sure whether she was relieved or disappointed that Omar wasn't on the same table as her. Out of the corner of her eye she saw that he and Amanda were sitting at a table on the far side of the room from her own. Maybe now, she thought, I can relax and enjoy the rest of the day.

Mike Collard, the hospital chaplain, said grace and after the guests were seated again the first course, of smoked salmon and asparagus tips, was served.

'That was a lovely ceremony,' said Penny, and there were nods of agreement from all the others except Guy.

'I think it was a bit close for comfort,' he said, and Jon and Gavin both laughed.

'Not thinking of making an honest woman of Julie yet, then, Guy?' asked Penny, and Sandie, remembering the conversation she'd recently had with Julie, threw her friend a quick, concerned glance, but now there was simply a look of resignation on her face.

'There's plenty of time for that,' said Guy in a shocked voice. 'People don't rush into things like that these days. Do they?' he added, glancing pleadingly round the table when no one answered.

'Not if they can help it,' said Jon lightly.

'It's different for Tom and Kate,' Guy went on. 'They've both been there before, and they have kids—but for those of us who haven't, it's another matter entirely. It's a big thing, what with the mortgage then the kids, sleepless nights and all that. And just when you think you might recover there are school fees, then the teenage years when I'm told even your car isn't your own any more.'

'Tell me about it,' said Gavin gloomily. 'And it doesn't end there. Our daughter's getting married next year and I'm thinking of taking out a second mortgage to pay for it all.'

'It all sounds horrendous,' said Jon.

'I reckon you and I have it right, Jon, don't you?' said Guy with a laugh.

'You mean having your cake and eating it?' said Sandie. She didn't know why she'd said it. She certainly hadn't meant to, but somehow she had been stung into the retort. There was a slightly awkward silence around the table then the waiter arrived to clear their dishes and the tension was broken.

The second course of lamb in rosemary sauce and fresh baby vegetables was followed by a dessert of passion fruit cheesecake and ice cream. The conversation became more varied as the wine flowed. Sandie noticed that Jon drank very little and was reminded of his intention to drive back to Chester that night. When he had given his reasons she had accepted and understood them, but now she felt a sudden surge of annoyance. Surely, for once, he could have made the effort to ensure he had the entire weekend off? Had it not mattered enough to him? With a frown she glanced up from her plate, only to find that Omar was looking at her from the far side of the room. As her gaze met his he inclined his head slightly and quickly she averted her eyes. Even if she had been relieved that he'd not been seated at her table, and she wasn't entirely certain of that, it seemed she was still to be aware of him even from the other side of the room.

Champagne was served after the meal and Matt, watched proudly by Louise, called the company to raise their glasses in a toast to Tom and Kate.

'Tom and Kate.' The acclamation echoed round the room then silence fell as Tom rose to his feet for his speech.

His words were poignant and touching, telling of how he'd settled for the single life once more until he'd become aware of the beautiful lady who worked alongside him each day, of hardly daring to ask her out, afraid of rejection, for all the world like any teenager on his first date instead of a mature man, then of his joy and elation when it had become apparent to him that Kate felt the same way. He spoke of the love he felt for his own children and his growing affection for Kate's, of how he had so missed family life and of how his life had now changed out of all recognition. He ended his speech by thanking everyone for coming to witness their promises to each other then thanking the lovely woman at his side for agreeing to be his wife and promising to spend the rest of her life with him.

'Oh,' said Penny, tears in her eyes as she groped for her champagne glass, 'that was lovely. I would never have expected that of Tom.'

Even Guy and Jon seemed subdued by the simple sincerity of Tom's speech and there was no trace of the cynicism they had shown earlier towards the state of matrimony.

Matt's speech, in complete contrast, was hilarious, full of medical anecdotes, which brought gales of laughter from the entire company. More photographs followed as the newlyweds cut the cake which was then served with coffee.

After the reception guests drifted onto the hotel terrace or into the bar where they congregated in little groups, chatting and relaxing, while others took a stroll in the gardens as the band, which had been hired to play for the evening, set up in the hotel's ballroom. Once again, in spite of her endeavours to the contrary, Sandie found herself acutely aware of Omar as he chatted in his easy style to other guests, Amanda continuously hanging not only on his arm but also onto his every word, gazing up into his eyes as she did so.

At one point in the ladies' powder room Sandie found herself in the company of Julie and Amanda as all three repaired their make-up and combed their hair.

'I think,' said Julie, her eyes meeting Sandie's in the long mirror above the hand-basins, 'that Guy found an ally in your Jon.'

'Seems that way,' Sandie replied with a little shrug. 'I don't think the word ''marriage'' features in their vocabulary.'

'Not like Omar, then,' said Amanda with a sigh, breaking into their conversation.

'Oh,' said Julie flippantly. 'Proposed, then, has he?'

For some reason Sandie found herself holding her breath.

'No, not exactly.' Amanda appeared to be taken aback by Julie's bluntness. 'But if I play my cards right I would say it will only be a matter of time.'

'You'll have to sort your divorce out first, then, won't you?' said Julie waspishly.

'That won't be a problem.' With her nose in the air Amanda left the powder room.

'I don't know what he sees in her,' said Julie with a sigh. 'Mind you, if what I've heard about Omar is correct he'll soon be moving onto the next one.'

When Sandie and Julie returned to the ballroom it was to find that Omar and Amanda had joined Guy and Jon. 'Looks like they've sorted out where we are sitting,' remarked Julie as they made their way across the dance floor.

Carefully avoiding eye contact with Omar, Sandie took a seat beside Jon, then Omar and Jon organised drinks and carried them back to the table from the bar. They had barely sat down when the band struck up with 'I Will Always Love You' and Tom and Kate took to the floor amidst applause from their guests.

After a while Matt and Louise joined the newlyweds on the floor and were soon joined by other couples. Jon stood up and, turning to Sandie, held out his hand. She rose and joined him, allowing him to lead her onto the floor, but as she did so she knew a moment's irritation at his assumption that she would want to dance—he hadn't even bothered to ask her. Had their relationship really become so predictable that each knew what the other would want? Some might think that was a good thing, she thought as Jon put his arms around her, that they knew each other so well that they could gauge one another's responses. Others might have called it taking one another for granted.

'Are you enjoying the day?' she asked him, as they slowly moved around the floor to the music.

'Yes,' he replied, 'It's been good.'

'So you're glad you came?'

'Of course.' There was a slight note of protest in his voice. 'Why wouldn't I be?'

'No reason.' She gave a little shrug. After a few moments she went on, 'When will we get to see each other again?'

'I don't know.' He shook his head. 'I'll have to see what I can work out. Mum's been pestering me about when the two of us are planning to go home again—seems like she's been getting together with your mum and planning some sort of family reunion.'

'Oh, dear,' said Sandie, then fell silent. The last thing she wanted at the present time was to have to make a trip to their home town and be forced to field a barrage of questions about when there would be a wedding and how many babies they intended having. Their respective families meant well, she knew that, and she guessed it was understandable that they were curious. After all, she and Jon had been going out together for as long as anyone could remember. But whereas in the past they had accepted all the good-natured interrogation, now for some reason she found it was the last thing she wanted, and she suddenly suspected, some-what surprisingly, that it was also the same for Jon. 'We'll have to think about it,' she said vaguely at last.

'Yes,' he agreed, and Sandie thought he sounded relieved. 'We'll think about it.' Over Jon's shoulder she suddenly caught a glimpse of Amanda's emerald green outfit and realised that she was dancing with Omar. Her arms were around his neck while his hands rested lightly on her back, below her waist. For some ridiculous reason, for Sandie the sight of his hands there on the woman's back, dangerously low, caused an unexpected throb of desire deep inside her. She tried to look away but found she couldn't. Then even as she stared, mes-merised, Omar lifted his head and over Amanda's shoulder and for the umpteenth time that day his gaze met hers and her heart turned over.

She and Jon stayed on the floor for another number then returned to their seats, only to get up again just moments later as the beat changed and people surged onto the floor.

Afterwards Sandie danced with Guy, then with Matt, then with Jon again, and it wasn't until after another fast and furious session where everyone took to the floor to dance to the music of the 1970s that the beat slowed. She'd returned to the table for a drink and when she looked up she found Omar standing in front of her.

'Sandie?' he said softly. 'My turn, I think?'

She nodded, set her glass down, stood up and, not daring to look at Jon—which was crazy when she considered that she'd danced with other men without batting an eyelid—allowed Omar to take her hand and lead her onto the dance floor.

It was a slow, sensual number and Omar led her right into the centre of the floor so they were in the midst of the other couples before he turned and, with a sigh which was barely perceptible, drew her into his arms. For Sandie it felt like coming home after a long, arduous journey, a journey made up of the moments they had shared since their first meeting, the exchanged confidences and all the glances that had passed between them, especially during the course of that day.

It was wrong, she knew that. Wrong to feel this way when the man she loved and with whom she imagined she would be spending the rest of her life was sitting only a few feet away. And she did love Jon, didn't she? Of course she did, she told herself fiercely. But as Omar's arms tightened around her she found herself doubting it. Surely if she was as much in love with Jon as she thought she was, or as she should be, then she wouldn't be feeling this way about another man.

'Sandie,' he murmured, 'I've wanted to do this all day.'

'Do what?' she asked, her eyes widening as she moved her head back in order to look into his eyes.

'Hold you,' he said softly, 'hold you close to me and hear your heart beating against mine.'

'Omar, don't,' she whispered. 'You mustn't say such things.'

'Why not?' he protested.

'Because of Amanda?' she began, only for him to dismiss the idea with a wave of his hand.

'She is perfectly happy, or haven't you noticed?' he said dismissively, and when Sandie looked over his shoulder she saw Amanda dancing with a doctor from Orthopaedics. Her arms were wound around his neck in exactly the same way she had danced with Omar.

'Well, Jon, then,' she added more firmly.

'Ah, Jon,' he said. 'Well, that's another story.'

'What do you mean?' she demanded, looking up at him again.

'Not now,' he said, his grip tightening again. 'Another time. Now, let us just enjoy the moment.'

She should have pursued it, demanded to know what he'd meant by his suggestion that somehow implied—what? That Jon didn't count in some way? That he was inconsequential? If that was the case, she should put him right. But somehow, no doubt tired from the events of the day and the effects of champagne, she couldn't summon the necessary energy and was content instead to rest her head on his shoulder and sway gently to the sexy rhythm of the music while at the same time wishing the moment could last for ever.

It didn't, of course, coming to an end as all such moments had to, but not until they had stayed on the floor for the duration of two numbers. And if she'd been aware of Omar's presence before, she was doubly aware of him afterwards, to such an extent that she could hardly bear to see him with Amanda.

At last the evening drew to a close and everyone gathered outside on the terrace to wave goodbye to Kate and Tom as they left for a secret destination. The guests began to disperse and it seemed in no time at all Sandie found herself in the back of a cab beside Jon, with Omar in front beside the driver as they drove back to Pitt's Place.

Jon only came inside briefly to change, after bidding Omar goodnight, then it was time for him to drive north back to Chester.

'I still think you should wait until the morning,' said Sandie.

'I can't,' he said apologetically. 'I'm on duty first thing. Don't worry, I'll get a few hours' sleep when I get back.'

She followed him down the wide staircase and outside onto the forecourt then, when they reached his sports car, he turned to her. 'It's been great, Sandie,' he said, enfolding her in his arms and looking down at her, 'really great.'

'Yes, Jon,' she agreed, 'it has.' His kiss was light, almost fleeting.

'I'll be in touch soon,' he said, releasing her and turning to open the car door.

'Yes.' She nodded. 'Take care, Jon,' she added, 'and drive carefully. Love you.'

'Me, too.' He smiled, started the engine and raised one hand, then he was gone, away down the drive until all she could see were the red taillights as he disappeared onto the road.

With a little sigh Sandie turned and walked back across the forecourt to the house, in darkness at this hour save for the security light that burned at the entrance. There had been no sign of Julie and Sandie guessed she must have gone to Guy's flat, where she sometimes stayed the night. She'd almost reached the entrance when suddenly someone standing in the shadows moved forward.

Sandie jumped, fear prickling the back of her neck, until the person spoke. 'It's all right, Sandie,' he said, 'it's only me.'

'Omar, you frightened the life out of me,' she said, aware that her heart was thumping even more now that she knew it was Omar. Maybe an intruder would have been easier.

'Whatever are you doing out here?' she added weakly.

'I came out for some air,' he said easily. 'I often do at this time of night. I like the silence and the night sky. It reminds me of— But never mind about that. I saw Jon go—I really thought he might change his mind about going tonight and wait until the morning.'

'I know,' Sandie agreed. 'So did I, but he said he had to get back because he's on an early shift in the morning.'

'I'm sure if that had been me, I would have arranged things a little differently.'

'Yes, well.' Sandie gave a helpless little gesture. 'You know what it's like with staff shortages and holidays and things…'

'Even so, if it had been me I would have taken some leave if it would have meant spending the night with you.'

'Omar…don't…' she began, but he carried on talking as if she hadn't spoken.

'He must be mad,' he said. 'There is no way on earth that I could have walked away from you tonight.'

'Omar, please…'

'If I were him, I would not have been able to wait to make love to you.'

'Omar!'

'I'm sorry, Sandie,' he said, 'but I have to say what I feel. You are a beautiful, desirable woman and your need for love is great. I could feel that when you were in my arms, when we danced together. You needed love tonight and your man has walked away from you. As I say, the man must be mad.'

While Sandie was still reeling from Omar's remarks and almost without her being aware of what was happening, he pulled her into his arms and brought his mouth down hard onto her own, leaving her gasping when equally abruptly he drew back while still continuing to hold her.

'And that's something else I've been want-ing to do all day,' he said. 'From the moment I saw you in that dress and that straw hat you were wearing, I wanted to do that.'

'You shouldn't,' she said, shaking her head. 'You mustn't, Omar...'

'Tell me you haven't also wanted that to happen?' He lowered his head slightly in order to look into her face under the overhead lamp.

'Sandie...?' he persisted when she didn't answer. 'No? Well, I'll tell you what I think. I think you wanted me to do that every bit as much as I wanted to. I've been aware of you all day, just as I know you have been aware of me. When we danced you melted in my arms...just like this...' Almost roughly he tightened his grip again. Pulling her closer, he once more covered her mouth with his own, but this time the touch of his lips was like liquid fire spreading through Sandie's veins and, completely unable to fight or resist him any further, she allowed her lips to part beneath his and gave herself up to the sheer thrill of being kissed by him.

CHAPTER SEVEN

IT FELT like heaven and Sandie found herself responding to Omar as every sense was heightened, every passion aroused and desire awakened in a way she had never known before. The fact that this was wrong was lost somehow in a roller-coaster ride of emotion as he moulded her body with his hands, drawing her even closer so that she was left in no doubt of his body's own response to what was happening between them. He covered her with kisses, not just her lips but her face, her eyelids, her neck and the vulnerable hollow between neck and shoulder which for Sandie brought fresh shafts of delight. And then, just as it would seem that he might take their passion to its inevitable conclusion either in his apartment or right there in the gardens with the wide starry sky above them, for Sandie the small still voice of reason intervened and she pulled away sharply. 'Omar,' she gasped, 'I can't do this... I'm sorry.'

He groaned and tried to pull her back into his arms. 'Why?' His voice was thick with desire, raw with emotion.

'Because it's wrong,' she said. 'I have Jon…'

'But do you love him?' With an intense effort Omar seemed to bring himself under control.

'Of course I do,' she protested. 'I've always loved Jon, ever since I was a little girl I've loved him…'

'And does he love you?'

'Yes,' she cried, 'of course he does.'

'Then he doesn't love you enough.' Omar stated flatly. 'If he did he would be here now, and it would be him holding you, loving you, and not me. I think,' he went on after a moment of silence, 'you need to look at this love you have for each other and ask yourself if it is the right sort of love.'

'What do you mean?' she demanded indignantly. 'Of course it's the right sort of love.'

'Does he make you feel the way you did just now when you were in my arms?' His voice was low now, seductively low, and his words brought a little shiver from Sandie, rendering her incapable of an answer. Deep in her heart she knew the answer—no one had ever made her feel the way she had for those brief moments in Omar's arms—but how could she admit that to him? To do so would surely bring about another moment of unbridled folly, and if it were to happen again Sandie doubted she would have the strength to resist him for a second time.

'I have to go,' she said, turning from him with a helpless little gesture and walking the short distance to the front entrance.

'You didn't answer my question,' he persisted.

'Omar, you have no right to question me in this way,' she said, fumbling with the catch on the front door.

'Is that because you know what I'm saying is right?' He was directly behind her, so close that she could feel his warm breath on the back of her neck. Desperately she turned the handle and the door at last swung open. With short, rapid steps she crossed the hall, her high-heeled shoes making loud clicking noises in the quiet of the night. He followed her up the staircase, so close that had she stopped and turned she would have tumbled straight into his arms. Somehow she resisted the impulse, knowing that should she give in to the temptation it would be her downfall, most likely the end of her relationship with Jon, with recriminations from their families and friends. And for what? Would it be worth it, a brief, passionate fling with Omar, who would no doubt tire of her just the way he had of others before moving on to another conquest? Of course it wouldn't. With an almost superhuman effort, as they reached the door to her apartment she turned to face him. 'Goodnight, Omar,' she said firmly.

'Not even a goodnight kiss?' There was almost a little-boy-lost expression on his face now, one which Sandie suspected had brought about the desired effect many times in the past.

'No,' she said equally firmly, 'not even that.'

'Not even a teeny one? And after such a perfect day?'

'No, Omar not even a teeny one.' She doubted there could be any such thing with Omar. If downstairs on the forecourt had been anything to go by, the most gentle, the most chaste, the most fleeting of kisses would rapidly escalate, spinning right out of control.

'Ah, well, maybe another time.' He held up his hands in defeat. 'Goodnight, Sandie.'

'Goodnight, Omar,' she said again, even more firmly this time, as she unlocked her door and stepped into her apartment.

'Think about what I said, won't you?' he said urgently as she would have shut the door. 'About you and Jon. Marriage is for life, Sandie. Life with the wrong person...' He shrugged, the sentence unfinished, but leaving Sandie in no doubt as to his meaning.

She shut the door and, with her eyes closed, leaned against it. Thank goodness she had somehow found the strength to resist him. If she hadn't, even now she would, no doubt, have been in his apartment and he would have been making love to her. And that was the last thing she wanted.

Wasn't it? she asked herself as she prepared for bed, stepping out of her shoes, peeling off the dress Omar had so admired. Of course it was, she told herself firmly, almost severely.

But if that was the case, why had she responded in the way she had to that magical

kiss—because that was what it had been, like
nothing she'd ever known before, involving
every part of her, every feeling and all her
senses. But wasn't that just Omar—his style,
his art of seduction? Didn't he pursue the same
line with every woman he tried to entice into
his bed? No doubt he did, so surely it was a
good thing that she'd somehow found the will
to walk away. If she hadn't, how dreadful she
would have felt afterwards in the cold light of
day when she would have been forced to face
reality.

With that thought uppermost in her mind,
Sandie turned out her bedroom light. Before
getting into bed, she drew back the curtains
and gazed out over the moonlit garden then up
at the wide, starry expanse of the sky. She was
sure that for a moment Omar had been about
to talk of starry skies in Africa but he had
stopped himself. Maybe she should have en-
couraged him to continue. Maybe if she had,
that was all they would have done, talked of
African skies and not ended up sharing those
moments of deep intimacy. That, she knew,
would have been far more sensible but at the
same time, perversely, she also knew she

didn't regret those moments—just as long as they weren't repeated. She knew she would treasure them and keep them locked away in some dark, secret corner of her heart. With a deep sigh she turned from the window and climbed into bed, willing herself to go to sleep immediately, afraid of the thoughts that might creep in if she didn't—thoughts that would inevitably involve the man lying in his own bed only yards away from her.

He had told her to examine her relationship with Jon. The thoughts flowed unbidden as the hands of her bedside clock showed one-thirty. But surely nothing had changed there. Jon was exactly the same as he had always been, and as for their relationship, well, wasn't that also the same? Hadn't they always seen each other infrequently, made love infrequently, and hadn't their plans for the future always been vague, with neither of them exerting undue pressure on the other? Wasn't that the way they liked it? By two o'clock she had convinced herself that, yes, of course it was, but after turning over for the umpteenth time she found other niggling thoughts creeping in. The way Jon had appeared indifferent to the marriage ceremony, the way he had sided with Guy in his remarks about avoiding marriage and then, in spite of her earlier acceptance of the facts, the way he hadn't stayed with her for the weekend. Had anyone else read anything into the situation, casting doubts on the strength of their relationship, or had it only been Omar. And if he had, was that purely and simply because he had wanted to seduce her? By two-thirty her thoughts were even more troubled and she found herself wondering about Omar's relationship with Amanda. Omar seemed casual about the whole thing but Amanda seemed quite possessive about him.

By three o'clock, desperate for sleep, she was questioning whether or not she could really love Jon when she had so enjoyed those moments in the arms of another man.

She must have slept eventually but when she awoke at seven to bright sunlight streaming through the open curtains she felt exhausted, and relieved that it was Sunday and she was off duty for another day.

'Dr Rawlings, can you come straight to SCBU, please?' said the voice on the other end of the phone.

'Of course,' Sandie replied. 'I'll be with you in a couple of minutes.' It was Monday morning and Sandie had only just reported for duty when her pager had gone off and the request had come through from the special care baby unit.

Probably for the first time in her life, she hadn't wanted to go to work that morning. It had nothing to do with the job itself and everything to do with not having to see a certain registrar. She had successfully avoided him the previous day, not going out until she had seen him drive away from Pitt's Place and returning before him, closing her door and not emerging again until this morning when it had been time to go to the hospital. It couldn't last, this avoidance of Omar, she knew that. While it might have worked at Pitt's Place for one day, there was no way it could work for long at Ellie's where their work continually placed them in each other's company. Even as she hurried to SCBU she found herself wondering whether he would be there.

He was the first person she saw as she stepped into the unit and went through the ritual of washing her hands, which Louise insisted on for anyone entering the unit. He was in conversation with Matt and both men looked up as she approached. Carefully she avoided Omar's gaze, focussing her attention on Matt.

'We have a problem, Sandie,' said Matt.

'Is it Augustus?' she asked anxiously.

'No.' Matt shook his head. 'There is actually a sign of improvement in Augustus today. No, this is a baby born at twenty-eight weeks—a little girl weighing less than two pounds. She has a heart defect, although at this moment we are uncertain about its extent. The cardiologist is on his way to see her now. I would like you to see her then to talk to the parents. I have to attend another birth so Omar will accompany you.'

'Very well.' Sandie nodded, grateful to Matt for being so aware that she needed all the experience she could glean for her work with premature babies. After Matt's departure she and Omar followed Louise to the high-dependency unit where the baby was in an incubator, a respirator enabling her to breathe, with tubes attaching her to a heart monitor and another nasal tube to administer nourishment and medication. The baby's parents were seated either side of the incubator, their faces drawn with worry, eyes heavy with tiredness.

Louise took control. 'This is our registrar, Dr Nahum,' she explained, 'and this is Dr Rawlings. They would like to take a look at baby Natasha.' Turning to Omar and Sandie, she said, 'These are Natasha's parents, Lizzie and Pete Simmonds.'

Nods and hellos followed then Lizzie spoke. 'She *is* going to be all right, isn't she?' she asked, and Sandie suspected it was the same question she levelled at every medic who crossed the threshold of the HDU.

'We very much hope so,' Omar replied. 'We have arranged for a consultant to come down and see Natasha a little later this morning, but before he comes Dr Rawlings and I want to examine her and carry out a few observations, just so that we'll be able to give him a completely up-to-date picture.'

'But you'll disturb her again,' protested Lizzie. 'She's only just closed her eyes. Do you have to do it?' Pleadingly she looked from Omar to Sandie then to the tiny form that lay in the incubator clad only in a minute nappy, a little pink hat, cotton mittens and a pair of bootees so tiny they would have fitted a doll.

'We must let the doctors do their job, love,' said her husband gently.

'But I can't bear it when they stick needles into her and upset her...' Tears trickled down Lizzie's cheeks and angrily she dashed them away.

'Why don't you and Pete come to my office and have a cup of coffee?' suggested Louise briskly.

'I shouldn't leave her...' In the midst of her exhaustion Lizzie threw another lingering glance at her daughter.

'She'll be fine,' said Louise. 'In the best possible hands. Come along. A little break will do you both good, then when the doctors have finished you can come back and be with Natasha when the consultant comes to see her.' Louise's persuasion was finally accepted, though it was with a certain amount of reluctance that Lizzie, together with her husband, followed Louise out of the room and across the special care unit to her office.

Together Omar and Sandie carried out the necessary observations and examination of the tiny baby who, as her mother had so rightly predicted, squirmed with indignation on being disturbed.

'The heartbeat is definitely erratic,' said Sandie, after listening carefully to the baby's chest, which was so small that the warmed head of her stethoscope covered the entire area.

'I'm glad Marcus Lichfield is on duty,' Omar replied, 'although I'm not sure that, should it prove to be necessary, even he will risk operating on such a tiny baby.'

'What do you think her chances are without surgery?' asked Sandie anxiously.

'Let's wait and see what the man himself says,' Omar replied, 'before we make any predictions.'

'But the signs aren't good, are they?' Reaching out one finger, Sandie gently touched the baby's cheek.

'No, they aren't,' Omar admitted. 'To be born this early and with such a low birth weight is enough of a handicap in itself, but to have a heart defect as well...' He trailed off, leaving Sandie in no doubt about his own thoughts on the baby's condition.

'We have a ward round to do.' Sandie would have moved away from the incubator but Omar stopped her, reaching out and lightly touching her arm. At the feel of his hand on her bare skin she froze in her tracks.

'I didn't see you yesterday,' he said softly.

'No,' she agreed. 'Under the circumstances I thought it better.'

'Sandie,' he said in the same low tones, 'we have to see each other. We work together, we live in the same building—it's inevitable. You can't go on avoiding me.' She didn't reply, continuing to stand very still and very silent, gazing down at the tiny form between them as it battled valiantly for its very existence. 'If I offended you last night,' Omar went on at last, 'I'm sorry, because it truly wasn't my intention. But somehow I don't think I did offend you. Sandie?' He lowered his head in an attempt to look into her face. 'Did I?'

She took a deep breath and looked at him, her heart twisting slightly at the expression in his eyes. 'No, Omar,' she admitted at last, 'you didn't offend me…but…we can't let it happen again,' she added desperately.

He shrugged. 'If you fear there's a danger of that, maybe you should be asking yourself why,' he said. Then, not giving her the chance to respond in any way, he added, 'Come, as you so rightly say, we have a round to do here. Then I have to be in Theatre, so I would appreciate it if you would give this little mite's parents some time.'

Together they left the HDU and, after joining up with Louise again, they proceeded to complete a round of the other babies on the special care unit. There were twelve babies in all besides Natasha. Most had been born prematurely and were on the unit so that they could receive special care until they reached a satisfactory weight and were feeding and breathing independently. Two had been born at full term but were on the care unit for other reasons—one had gone home and picked up a respiratory infection, and the other had gastric problems.

By the time Omar and Sandie had completed the round, examining the babies and changing medication, treatment procedures and feeding patterns where necessary, it was time for Omar to leave for Theatre. When

Sandie returned to Louise's office she found that Marcus Lichfield, the cardiologist, had examined baby Natasha and was just leaving the unit.

'What did he say?' asked Sandie anxiously as the doors closed behind him.

'It was as we feared,' Louise replied. 'She has a hole in the heart but he thinks she is too small to survive surgery. He has said he will review the case when she is six weeks old.'

'Presuming she reaches six weeks,' said Sandie quietly.

'Exactly.' Louise nodded. 'Needless to say, Lizzie and Pete are in a bit of a state. Would you go and have a chat with them?'

'Of course,' Sandie replied. 'I was going to go and see them again anyway.'

She found Pete and Lizzie Simmonds beside their daughter. Lizzie was weeping in Pete's arms while Pete himself looked up helplessly at Sandie, the anguish in his eyes there for anyone to see.

'That's right,' said Sandie, gently touching Lizzie's shoulder, 'have a good cry, then you have to conserve your energy for the fight ahead.'

'What fight?' Lizzie lifted her head and looked at Sandie through her tears.

'Why, the fight for your daughter's life, of course. She's too tiny to do all the fighting herself, you know, and who better than her parents to fight for her?'

'Mr Lichfield says she's too small to operate on,' said Pete.

'At the moment, maybe,' Sandie agreed, 'but she'll grow. She won't always be this size, you know.'

'But she has this hole in her heart,' protested Lizzie. 'What if she doesn't get any bigger…? What if…?' Her voice choked and tears flowed afresh down her cheeks.

'It didn't sound as if he held out much hope,' said Pete, and his voice was husky with unshed tears. 'In fact, when we suggested it, he agreed it would be sensible to have her baptised…'

'Well, yes, that's fine, it's a lovely thing to do,' said Sandie enthusiastically. 'We have our own chaplain here at the hospital. He often baptises babies.'

'Do any of those babies ever make it?' asked Pete, and Lizzie raised her head again, desperate to hear Sandie answer yet at the same time fearful of knowing.

'Oh, yes,' said Sandie firmly, 'of course they do. Special Care here at Ellie's is second to none.'

'Even if a baby has problems like Natasha's?' whispered Lizzie.

'Even that,' Sandie replied. 'I absolutely believe the old saying of, "Where there's life there's hope." And your little Natasha is very much alive. So, we are all going to fight for her, right?' She looked from Pete to Lizzie then back to Pete again.

'Yes, of course we are.' Pete still sounded a little uncertain and glanced at his wife. 'Lizzie?' he said.

'Yes,' she whispered. Drawing herself up, she brushed away her tears and took a deep breath, as if bracing herself for the battle ahead. Looking down at her tiny daughter, she said, 'We'll fight for you, little one, every inch of the way.'

Sandie swallowed. 'That's better,' she said. 'Now, shall I phone the chaplain and ask him to come in so that you can arrange this christening?'

*　　*　　*

'It's heartbreaking,' she said later to Penny on her return from SCBU as the two of them shared a pot of tea in the staffroom. 'Honestly, some of these situations just tear you apart.'

'So, this baby, is there much hope for her?' asked Penny as she sipped her tea.

'Not really.' Sandie shook her head. 'But I feel it's so important for the parents to feel they are fighting along with the staff and with the baby herself, and then if or when something happens they will at least feel as if they did everything possible and not spend the rest of their lives reproaching themselves. At the moment they are planning her baptism.'

'They don't see that as a negative step—like there's no hope?' asked Penny.

'I tried to make them see that it was something positive they could do for their daughter, and I'm sure Mike Collard was able to help them even more.'

'When's it to be?' asked Penny.

'At one-thirty.' Sandie glanced at her watch. 'I'm going to try to slip back to SCBU before I go to the outpatients clinic this afternoon.' She paused, nibbling a digestive biscuit. 'Is all well on the children's ward?'

Penny nodded. 'Matt did the round this morning—we knew you and Omar were in SCBU. Gemma has gone home and Lewis is due back tomorrow to start the next round of his treatment.'

'What about Sam?'

'Yes, he's doing fairly well—although we've had a bit of difficulty with pain control.'

'I'll come in to the ward after I've finished the clinic.'

'The wedding was lovely, wasn't it?' said Penny with a sigh.

'Yes, it was,' Sandie agreed. 'Do we know where Kate and Tom have gone?'

'Paris, apparently.'

'Wonderful,' said Sandie with a little sigh.

There was silence for a while then tentatively Penny spoke again. 'Sandie,' she began, 'I was wondering, about you and Jon…'

'What about me and Jon?' asked Sandie. She spoke lightly but for some reason she felt her muscles tense.

'Well, I'm not sure really.' Penny hesitated. 'But I've known you and Jon for a long time and, well, I don't know quite how to say this, but this time, at the wedding, you didn't seem to be so together as you usually are, if you get what I mean...' She trailed off uncertainly and when Sandie remained silent she went on, 'Oh, Sandie, I'm sorry, I shouldn't have said anything—don't take any notice of me.'

'No, it's all right, Penny,' Sandie replied slowly. 'Don't worry.'

'But it's none of my business even if there is anything wrong. You should just have told me to—'

'Actually, you're right,' Sandie heard herself say. 'Things aren't quite as they used to be between Jon and me.'

'Even so—'

'No, don't worry about it. Maybe I've been deluding myself that everything is OK when I should be examining our relationship a little more closely.'

'But you have been aware of it?' asked Penny anxiously.

'When I was up in Manchester, I noticed a change in Jon—a sort of vagueness or coolness, call it what you will, but I didn't really think it was anything too much to worry about.'

'And when he came down for the wedding he didn't stay over, did he?'

'No.' Sandie shook her head.

'And that isn't like Jon,' Penny observed.

'No, it isn't,' Sandie agreed. 'In fact, if I'm honest, he couldn't wait to get back. Oh, I know he said he had shifts but we all know that shifts can be changed, and it wasn't as if he didn't know about this wedding in advance, for heaven's sake.' She fell silent again, staring into her mug, then, looking up at Penny, she said, 'Are you trying to tell me that you think Jon might have somebody else?'

'Actually, no,' Penny replied. 'In fact, quite the reverse.'

'What do you mean?' Sandie frowned.

'I was thinking that Jon might be thinking that you may have somebody else.'

Sandie stared at Penny. 'What do you mean?' she said at last. 'Why would he think that?'

'Oh, no reason.' Penny looked embarrassed now, as if she wished she'd never started this particular conversation. 'Take no notice—it was just me being silly.'

'No, Penny, please. I want to know what you mean.'

'I told you, it's nothing,' Penny protested.

'It must have been something for you to have said it in the first place.'

'Well...it's just that I wondered if Jon might have picked up something between you and Omar, that's all...' Penny trailed off unhappily.

Sandie swallowed then, lifting her chin, said, 'What would he have picked up?'

'Well, you and Omar did seem rather close at the wedding.'

'I don't know what you mean,' Sandie protested.

'And in the evening, when you were dancing...'

'What about when we were dancing? I danced with lots of people and so did Omar. And he was with Amanda, for heaven's sake.'

'Maybe so,' replied Penny, 'but Omar only had eyes for you, Sandie, and I wasn't the only one who noticed.'

'What do you mean?' Sandie stared at her in dismay.

'Mary Payne and Melissa from Maternity noticed it and commented on it to me. All I'm saying is that if they noticed then there's a very good chance that Jon may have noticed.' When Sandie didn't immediately reply, searching desperately for a suitable denial, Penny spoke again. 'Omar Nahum is a very attractive man, Sandie, but he's also a heartbreaker. You and Jon have something really good going for you. I would hate to see you throw it all away only to get hurt at the end of it.' Penny drained her cup and stood up. 'This won't do,' she said with a sigh. 'I must get back to the ward—I'll see you later.'

'Yes,' said Sandie faintly. 'See you later.'

After Penny had gone, she sat for a while cradling her mug in her hands and thinking about what she had said. It had come as something of a shock to hear Penny say that others had noticed something between herself and Omar—in her naïvety she had imagined that she and Omar himself had been the only ones aware of that spark or whatever it was that had flared between them. Had Jon noticed? Penny had suggested he might have, and that that could be a possible reason for his coolness, although somehow she found herself doubting that was the case. She'd been aware of that coolness long before the wedding. It was probably nothing—tiredness or overwork. What really concerned her was that others at the hospital might think there was something between herself and Omar when quite clearly there wasn't. Rumours started that way, and that was something she could really do without. If it came to it, she would have to scotch any such rumours before they got out of hand, or get Omar to.

Finishing her own tea, she too stood up. Fleetingly the thought entered her head that Omar might not be bothered about any such rumours and consequently might not be too concerned with quashing them. Surely, though, he wouldn't want Amanda to hear gossip like that? With a frown she washed her mug, wondering as she did so just how important Amanda was to Omar. If he really cared about her, would he have kissed her, Sandie, in the way he had? Or were the rumours about him being some sort of serial heartbreaker really true?

Since Saturday night she had tried to put all thoughts of that kiss right out of her mind but she was finding that it would be right there, slipping back into her thoughts with alarming regularity. If only she didn't have to see him quite so often, it might have been easier to simply forget the whole thing. But there was no chance of that for he was there in her world whichever way she turned.

Leaving the staffroom, Sandie made her way back to SCBU where she found that Mike Collard had just arrived to baptise Natasha. Louise was also there, together with Lizzie, Pete and Lizzie's mother. Sandie slipped quietly into the back of the room, almost unnoticed in the emotion-charged atmosphere, and as Mike began the first prayer of the ceremony she felt a slight movement at her side. Turning her head, she found Omar beside her.

The service, although brief, was poignant and very moving, and when at last Mike leaned over the incubator and made the sign of the cross on the baby's tiny forehead, welcoming her into the church, Sandie doubted that tears were far away for anyone in the room, including herself. She blinked rapidly then started as she felt Omar take her hand and squeeze it tightly before releasing it. It happened so suddenly and was over so quickly that afterwards Sandie was to wonder if she had imagined it, but at the time her only concern was that someone else might have noticed. The last thing she wanted was for there to be anything to fuel the speculation that Penny had indicated had already started, but when she glanced quickly around she was relieved to notice that everyone's attention was focussed on little Natasha and no one seemed to have noticed anything untoward between the medics.

CHAPTER EIGHT

FOLLOWING the baptism, Sandie and Omar hurried to Outpatients where there was to be a paediatric clinic. 'This is getting to be quite a habit,' remarked Omar as, side by side, he and Sandie walked the corridors from the special care unit to the hospital's large outpatient department.

'What is?' Sandie threw him a sidelong glance.

'Me comforting you at moving lifetime events,' he replied.

'I always want to cry at something like that,' Sandie replied. 'I'm sorry,' she added.

'Don't be sorry.' He smiled. 'It means I get to be closer to you, even if it is only for a short time.'

'Omar…' she began warningly.

'All right, I know.' He held up his hands in a gesture of surrender. 'I shouldn't even be thinking in that way. You have Jon…'

'Yes,' Sandie agreed. As they turned the corner and entered Outpatients they saw Amanda standing at the desk, talking to the receptionist. 'And you have Amanda,' she murmured.

'Ah, yes, Amanda. So I have,' Omar murmured back, and Sandie couldn't immediately decide whether his comment held resignation or regret, or maybe even a bit of both. But whatever it was, it brought a smile to both their faces.

Amanda turned and caught sight of them at that moment. While she could not possibly have heard what had passed between them, the look on her face when she saw that they were smiling was one of suspicion, as if she imagined that she had been the object of their mirth. Which, in a way, Sandie supposed, she had, but not in a malicious way—that was the last thing she wanted. While in her deepest and darkest thoughts when she had pictured them together, she might have been jealous of Amanda with Omar, she would never have willingly given Amanda cause for anxiety.

'Is there anything wrong?' Amanda demanded frostily, looking from one to the other.

'No,' said Sandie quickly. 'No, of course not.'

'So was it a private joke or can we all share it?'

'There was no joke,' said Omar truthfully, 'simply an observation. I understand we have a full clinic so we won't delay any further.' Gently, in passing, he touched Amanda's cheek and deep inside Sandie felt something twist, some emotion that she doubted even had a name. Amanda, although still looking as if she doubted the explanation, settled for the gesture of affection from Omar, turning away with a self-satisfied little smile playing around her mouth.

Matt had already arrived and on that day, together with Omar, would see new patients awaiting diagnosis while Sandie would see patients on appointments following up either surgery or courses of treatment.

The list was long and covered the usual wide variety of paediatric cases, from children recovering from broken bones, tonsillectomies, appendicectomies and hernia repairs to skin allergies, gastric disorders and respiratory diseases like asthma and bronchitis. In some cases the parent or parents accompanying the child were still concerned over some aspect of the treatment, usually the fact that the condition did not seem to be responding to the treatment. In most cases Sandie was able to reassure and persuade that all that was needed was patience and perseverance.

There was one child that afternoon who proved to be the exception, however, and that was a little girl called Sophia. Sophia was the daughter of Angelo and Maria Fabiano who ran a restaurant in Franchester, which had long been a favourite with staff at Ellie's. Sophia was accompanied by her mother and smiled shyly when she saw Sandie. She had originally been referred to the hospital by her GP, suffering from severe eczema, and had been seen by consultant paediatrician Suzanne Purcell, who had prescribed steroid creams to be used in conjunction with wraps and antihistamines after first establishing what Sophia was allergic to.

'She's no better, Dr Sandie,' stated Maria flatly. 'We've done everything that Miss Purcell said but still she scratch—every night she scratch, scratch, scratch.'

'I see from the notes that Miss Purcell established that a wheat allergy may be the problem,' said Sandie as Maria began to loosen the wraps covering Sophia's legs and arms.

'We stop the wheat,' complained Maria. 'Nothing. Still she itch.'

'Then maybe we have to be looking for a different source,' replied Sandie, leaning forward to examine the little girl. The eczema was indeed extensive, red and flaking, and in some areas the skin was broken and looked infected. 'Hmm,' said Sandie, 'Miss Purcell isn't here today so I'm going to let Dr Omar take a look at this. Just wait a moment. He's only in the next room, I'll fetch him.' Leaving Sophia with her mother, Sandie left the room then knocked lightly on the door of the room where Omar was seeing his own list of patients. He bade her enter, she slipped into the room and found him alone. When he looked up and saw her, no one could have doubted the way his face lit up.

'Sandie,' he said softly, 'have you finished your list?'

She shook her head, trying hard to ignore the tenderness in his eyes. Surely he shouldn't be looking at her in that way—hadn't they agreed that, for heaven's sake?

'No, Omar,' she replied, 'I haven't finished. I have Sophia Fabiano who's come in for a follow-up appointment. She saw Suzanne six months ago with long-term atopic eczema, which she's suffered from since she was a baby. Suzanne established a wheat allergy and prescribed steroid creams to use with wraps and antihistamine syrup. Neither appears to be working at the moment. She has suffered several recent flare-ups and certain patches have become infected. I would like to prescribe an antibiotic for the infection and to arrange for further tests. I would also like to try another cream, which has achieved very good results in recent trials, but I need you to authorise it as Suzanne isn't here today.'

'Very well.' Omar stood up. 'I'll come and see her.'

Maria was ecstatic at seeing Omar, whom she knew well from his regular attendance at the restaurant.

'Hello, Maria, hello, Sophia.' Omar sat down beside them and began to carefully examine the child's limbs. 'Dr Rawlings wants to change Sophia's medication,' he said after a moment.

'Who is Dr Rawlings?' asked Maria in apparent bewilderment. When Omar half turned to Sandie, she laughed. 'Oh, you mean Dr Sandie. Now, if you'd said Dr Sandie, I would have known. I don't know this Dr Rawlings.'

'Well, like I say, Dr Sandie wants to change Sophia's medication,' Omar went on. 'She is going to prescribe an antibiotic to clear up this infection, and she wants you to try a different cream, this time without the wraps, to see if it will stop all this itching.' He smiled at the little girl who smiled back. Turning back to Maria, he said, 'We would also like you to bring Sophia in for some more tests just to see what else she may be allergic to.'

'You mean she not allergic to wheat?' demanded Maria. 'You mean we avoid this for nothing?' She threw her hands up in the air.

'Not necessarily,' Omar replied. 'It may be that wheat is only one of the things she is allergic to—there may well be others, possibly many others. There are even some theories that it may be related to stress, that while stress may not actually be the cause it could aggravate the situation. Can you think of anything that may be doing that?' he added casually.

'Maybe,' Maria replied guardedly. 'I see about it,' she added.

'Good.' Omar stood up. 'I'll leave you with Dr Sandie now and she'll give you a prescription.'

After he had gone Sandie wrote out the required prescription. 'Take that to the hospital pharmacy, Maria,' she said, tearing off the sheet and handing it to the child's mother. 'They may not have the cream in stock but if they haven't they will order it for you.'

'All right, Dr Sandie.' Maria stood up. 'And thank you,' she added.

'Well, let's hope we have hit upon something that may work.' Sandie smiled at Sophia who smiled back.

'Maybe we see you soon at the restaurant,' said Maria. 'We've missed you,' she added. 'They said you were away.'

'That's right.' Sandie herself stood up and, walking to the door, opened it for Maria. 'I was on a course in Manchester.'

'Ah,' said Maria knowingly, 'so near your Dr Jon, yes?' Maria and her husband were renowned for knowing about every relationship at Ellie's and even a few that others seemed unaware of.

'Yes.' Sandie nodded. 'Yes, I was.'

'Ah, I think I can hear more wedding bells—yes?' Maria laughed.

'Oh, I don't know about that,' Sandie replied. 'One wedding at a time for Ellie's is quite enough.'

'Did you catch Kate's bouquet on Saturday?'

'No,' Sandie replied with a laugh, 'I didn't.'

'Well, no matter.' Maria shrugged. 'It is only—what you say—an old woman's tale?'

'An old wives' tale,' Sandie corrected her. 'That's what we call it—an old wives' tale that whoever catches the bride's bouquet is to be the next bride.'

'Who did catch it?' asked Maria curiously.

'Er...I think it was Amanda Cromer,' Sandie replied. 'You know—she's a secretary here?'

'Huh.' Maria sniffed. 'She already have a husband, she have no business to be catching bouquets.'

'I believe they are separated,' Sandie murmured, remembering all too clearly the awful, inexplicable pang she had felt when Amanda had caught the bouquet, and the good-natured teasing of Omar by the other guests which had followed.

'Like I say, she have a husband,' said Maria. 'I hear she after our lovely Dr Omar...' she added darkly, almost as if uncannily she had been able to read Sandie's thoughts.

'Maria, I must get on,' said Sandie uncomfortably. It was one thing to chat to Maria about herself, but when the conversation started straying into the realms of the relationships of other members of staff it was another thing altogether.

'OK.' With an exaggerated gesture Maria and Sophia were gone, leaving Sandie to go back into her room and write up her reports on the afternoon's clinic. But somehow she found as she worked the whole thing seemed to be taking much longer than it should as snippets of her conversation with Maria kept popping into her head and refusing to leave.

At last she pushed the papers away and sat back in her chair, trying to identify what aspect of the conversation it was that was bothering her so much. Was it the bit about Amanda catching Kate's bouquet and everyone laughingly teasing that she and Omar would be the next couple to tie the knot? That *had* bothered her certainly. But it wasn't only that—there was something else. She frowned, trying to recall exactly what else had been said. It had been more to do with her than with Amanda—or even Omar, come to that. So what was it?

Maria had said she had missed seeing her in the restaurant and she had said she'd been away. Maria had asked where, and she had said Manchester, then Maria had assumed that she had been near Jon—yes, it was something to do with that. Maria had gone on to ask whether soon there might be more wedding bells—hers and Jon's—and she had evaded the question. Why had she done that?

At one time she would have laughingly agreed, but now she realised with a slightly sinking feeling that she no longer wanted to contemplate a wedding with Jon.

For a long while she sat staring with unseeing eyes at the papers on the desk as the truth washed over her then finally sank in. She loved

Jon, she'd always loved him, but she didn't want to marry him. The love she felt for him was the love of friends, maybe the love between a brother and a sister, not the sort of love that should be there between husband and wife. The sudden ringing of the phone on the desk jolted her out of her reverie and as she leaned forward and picked up the receiver she found that such was the enormity of her realisation her hands were shaking.

'Sandie?' It was Penny. 'Have you finished your clinic?'

'Yes, I'm just entering up notes,' she replied, surprised to find that her voice sounded quite normal.

'When you've finished, could you come to the ward, please?'

'Yes, of course.'

Fifteen minutes later she made her way to the children's ward, still disturbed by what she had discovered and wanting to get away somewhere quiet and on her own where she could analyse this startling conclusion and all its implications more fully.

The outward appearance of the ward was exactly as it always was: one of noisy, delightful muddle. Children played, the television was on in one corner while pop music played in another, parents chatted together, a baby was crying and all the while the staff did their best to carry out their duties with the minimum of fuss and disruption.

Penny was in her office and she looked up as Sandie knocked then pushed open the door.

'You wanted me?' asked Sandie.

'Come in, Sandie,' Penny replied, 'and close the door.'

'That sounds ominous,' said Sandie. 'Don't tell me, you want me to stay on and do an extra shift.'

'No.' Penny shook her head. 'It's nothing like that.'

It was only as Sandie sat down and peered at her friend that she saw Penny was upset. 'What is it?' she asked. 'There's something wrong, isn't there?'

'Yes, Sandie, I'm afraid there is. There isn't any easy way of saying this and I know you'll be upset…'

Sandie stared at her friend as she struggled to find the words she needed to say. 'It's the baby, isn't it?' she said. 'It's Natasha? She didn't make it. You know, I had this awful feeling she wasn't going to but, well, you hope, don't you? And when Mike baptised her I prayed that in spite of all the odds being so stacked against her she would pull through—'

'No, Sandie,' Penny stopped her, 'it isn't Natasha.'

'What?' Sandie stared at her again. 'Not Natasha?' she said hopefully.

'No, not Natasha.'

'Then what...who?'

'I'm sorry, Sandie, but it's Lewis.'

'Lewis...?' She continued to stare at Penny, not quite taking in what she was saying, then as Penny nodded, tears glistening in her eyes, she said stupidly, 'But it can't be, he went home...'

'Only to spend time with his family before the next lot of treatment started. His GP phoned,' Penny went on to explain as Sandie sank down onto a chair. 'He said that Lewis died peacefully in his sleep in the early hours of this morning. All his family were with him.'

As Penny's words sank in Sandie's shoulders slumped. 'Oh, why is life so unfair?' she demanded in anguish.

'The scan did show that the cancer was back alarmingly,' said Penny.

'Yes, I know,' Sandie said. A lump had arisen in her throat and the tears already prickled threateningly in her eyes. 'But I thought another course of chemo, maybe some radiotherapy...'

'He couldn't take any more,' said Penny, reaching out and taking a couple of tissues from a box on her desk, handing one to Sandie before blowing her own nose. 'He was a little fighter right to the end, but he'd had as much as he could take. I...I just wanted to tell you before you heard it from anyone else.'

'Thanks, Penny.' Sandie wiped her eyes. 'I appreciate that.'

'I don't know how we're going to tell Sam.' Penny looked through the glass partition towards the boy's bed and the empty one alongside. 'He was making all sorts of plans for when Lewis came back. I think I'll have a word with his parents first and see how they would like the matter broached.' She paused. 'Are you all right, Sandie?' she asked.

'I think I'll just take five minutes to get myself together,' Sandie replied. Without another word, with her head down, she left the sister's office and headed for the comparative sanctuary of the sluice room.

Burying her face in a towel, for a few minutes she allowed the tears to flow for the brave little boy whose courage had been an example to them all. Ever since Sandie had begun her training it had affected her deeply when a patient died, but never more so than when it was a child who should have had their whole life before them. She had learnt from bitter experience that the only way to come to terms with these feelings of grief was to give vent to them, even if it was only for a short space of time, because by bottling them up she had found that she suffered more in the long run.

She didn't hear the door of the sluice room open, was unaware that anyone had come into the room until she felt strong arms go around her. She started and lowered the towel, turning her head to find Omar's face only inches from her own.

'Omar,' she gasped. 'Oh, I'm sorry. I didn't hear you come in...'

'It's all right,' he said. 'Have a good cry. It's best to release the emotion.'

'Yes...I know...' Desperately she wiped her eyes, trying to get her tears under control, but somehow they just kept coming. 'But Lewis... Poor little boy... It's just so unfair...'

'I know,' he said soothingly. 'Life is unfair sometimes, Sandie, you know that.'

'I know.' She sniffed, suddenly aware of how frightful she must look, how red her nose would be. 'I should be used to this sort of thing by now,' she said, thinking that it was high time he released her but at the same time somehow pleased that he hadn't. It felt warm and comforting with his arms around her. 'Honestly, I call myself a doctor and I fall apart the moment someone dies. It's always the same. Every time I tell myself I need to toughen up and not let it get to me, but every time it happens... Maybe I'm in the wrong job,' she ended helplessly.

'Of course you're not,' said Omar firmly, his grip tightening slightly around her. 'You show tremendous compassion and I think that's an admirable trait in a doctor and certainly not something to be ashamed of. I also happen to think it's a good thing that you are able to let the emotion go. So often you hear of doctors bottling up all that emotion they are required to deal with and they end up with an overload of stress resulting in a nervous breakdown.'

'Yes, but…I've been trained…'

'Sandie, doctors are only human. I think the public overlooks that fact at times. We have the same reactions and emotions as everyone else yet we are expected to override them.'

'Maybe you're right,' she said, 'but now I've let it go, I need to pull myself together and get back to work.' She made as if to pull away from him but he still held her against him, so close that she could hear the beating of his heart through the fabric of his white coat.

'Sandie,' he murmured at last, his mouth against her hair, and just for a moment she relaxed against him, imagined what it would be like if there were no obstacles between them. There was no telling what might have happened next, in that moment when their emotional barriers were weakened, had the door of the sluice not opened and Penny came into the room. Sandie pulled sharply away from Omar and, hastily excusing herself, pushed past Penny without establishing eye contact and hurried off the ward to the doctors' staffroom.

Over the next few days Sandie gave much time and thought to what she was going to do about her relationship with Jon. It had taken her a little while to accept the fact that she no longer wanted to continue the relationship, let alone marry him and spend the rest of her life with him. She had to ask herself whether or not Omar had anything to do with these realisations and finally reached the conclusion that meeting him had been the trigger, that she did have feelings for the handsome registrar—feelings of such strength and complexity, feelings she had never had for Jon—and it was those that had made her question her relationship with Jon and find it wanting. Whether or not her feelings for Omar would prove lasting and whether in the cold light of day he would be interested in her if she were free were different matters altogether—maybe he was one of those men whose enjoyment came from reaching for the unattainable. And then, of course, there was Amanda. Sandie still didn't feel she wanted to be responsible for ending Omar's relationship with her. But all that would have to wait, she told herself firmly. First and foremost and by far the most important thing was to arrange to see Jon. There was no way she could end their relationship with the casualness of a phone call. Neither did she feel she could take the coward's way out and write a letter. The only thing to do was to arrange a meeting.

It was while she was trying to work out the details of such a meeting, whether or not she should go to Chester or whether Jon could come down again, that she received a phone call that decided the matter for her.

It was during one evening at Pitt's Place. The phone rang and Sandie lifted the receiver, expecting it to be Penny, who had said she would phone with details of a function which was shortly to be held at the hospital social club. But it wasn't Penny.

'Hi, Sandie.'

'Jon?' She gripped the receiver a little more tightly. She had already decided that she would phone him later that evening and here he was phoning her. 'Is everything all right?'

'Yes, of course.' He paused. 'And with you?'

'Yes, fine. I was going to phone you later.'

'Oh, were you?' Another pause. 'Listen, Sandie, I was wondering… I need to see you…'

'Oh, really? That's funny because I was going to say the same thing.'

'Oh?' He sounded surprised.

'Yes. What do you suggest?'

'Well, I'm not sure that I can get down again so soon. What I was wondering was whether or not we could meet somewhere at the weekend—say Sunday, perhaps about halfway. Oxford or somewhere. What do you think?'

'Yes, that sounds OK. I am off duty on Sunday and it is a bit far to come all the way to Chester just for a day. Yes, Oxford would be fine. How about we meet for lunch at that pub where we went before—you know, with your sister and her friends?'

'Yes, fine.' Jon sounded relieved. 'I really do need to see you, Sandie.'

'Likewise,' she said. 'There was no time to talk at the wedding.'

'No, quite,' he agreed. 'Until Sunday, then, about midday?'

'Yes, fine. Bye, Jon.'

'Bye, Sandie.'

As she hung up Sandie found herself wondering just what it was that Jon needed to see her about so urgently. Maybe he, too, thought their relationship had run its course and was going nowhere. On the other hand, what if he had finally plucked up the courage and intended asking her to marry him, to name a date for their wedding? He'd given no indication of that the previous weekend but could it be that Kate's and Tom's wedding had made him think and reassess his own life? Was he thinking it was high time they settled down, found somewhere to live and thought about having a family? And wasn't that what she had wanted until a very short time ago? At one time she would have been delighted at the very thought of such a thing, in all the planning, the telling of family and friends and the basking in their reactions and congratulations. Now the very idea of all that simply left her cold. Surely it wasn't only because of Omar that her feelings had changed so much, she told herself. Maybe not, but maybe it had been Omar who had made her finally realise that being married to the wrong man was something not worth contemplating.

But how would she cope with Jon if that was the object of their meeting? She had no idea, she only knew it had to be done. She decided she would tell no one of the proposed meeting, not Julie, not Penny and certainly not Omar. If she did, she was sure there would be reactions and advice to deal with and she wasn't sure she could cope with either, well meaning as they might be. Julie would tell her to go for it if Jon proposed, that it was hard enough to get any man to settle down these days, while Penny would urge caution if she told her she was intending to end the relationship, to think very carefully about what she was giving up, that she and Jon had a lot of history and it would be foolish in the extreme to throw all that away for…for what? A whim, that Jon may not after all be the right man? She could hardly tell them how Omar had made her feel. They would simply laugh at her, tell her to pull herself together and get on with her life, that Omar made a career of breaking hearts and that that was exactly what he would do to hers. And what of Omar himself? What would he say if she told him she was meeting Jon? Would he tell her to follow her heart or her head? She had no idea. She only knew she had no intention of finding out, which made it all the more difficult when on Sunday morning she prepared to leave Pitt's Place for Oxford and found to her dismay that her car wouldn't start.

'Are you having trouble?'

She looked up to find Omar beside the car. 'I think it's the battery,' she replied. 'It's completely flat.'

'Can I give you a lift anywhere?' he asked.

'I was going to Oxford to meet Jon.' She glanced at her watch. 'I may just be able to catch him before he leaves Chester to tell him not to come.'

'Don't do that,' said Omar quickly. 'I'll take you if you like.'

'All the way to Oxford?' She stared at him. 'No, Omar, I couldn't possibly expect you to do that, and on your day off as well.'

He shrugged. 'I don't have anything else to do and while you are with Jon I could visit my grandparents—a visit is overdue. They live at Woodstock, just north of Oxford.'

She stared at him. This was not at all what she had planned.

'Just give me ten minutes and I'll be with you,' he said. Then, not waiting to hear any further protest, he turned and disappeared into the house, leaving Sandie staring after him.

Moments later he reappeared and unlocked his own car, and after only a moment's hesitation with a little sigh she slid into the seat beside him.

CHAPTER NINE

IT WAS one of those glorious mornings when the sky still retained the intense blue of summer but the first nip of autumn was in the air, with its promise of log fires and cosy evenings, when the trees were on the turn, competing with each other in a contest of vibrant colours, when dew lingered on garden lawns and cobwebs glistened on gateposts and hedgerows.

For Sandie, as they sped through country lanes between hedges thick with berries and hips, it felt so utterly right to be sitting there beside Omar that she gave up trying to justify her reasons for accepting his offer of transport. Maybe sensing the importance of this unexpected meeting with Jon, he respected her wish to remain silent, instead comparing the English countryside in autumn to that of Somalia, knowing his comments needed no response from her.

'The sunsets were incredible,' he told her, 'the sun like a huge ball of molten gold in a sky so vast it is unimaginable, sinking slowly beneath the horizon and followed immediately by darkness and a sudden drop in temperature. Once,' he went on, 'I visited the Serengeti in Tanzania and joined a safari. The wildlife was wonderful. I saw elephant and giraffe, lions and gazelles, all coming to drink from the same waterhole at dawn, and from a small aircraft I watched the huge migration of wildebeest across the plains. That, I think, was the most unbelievable sight of all.'

'It sounds wonderful,' said Sandie with a little sigh, staring out of the window as they passed fields, some lush and green, where sheep and cattle grazed beside streams, and others rich and brown, already ploughed for the next year's crops.

'Yes,' he agreed, 'it was, and I believe a part of me is still there in that land of my father.'

It wasn't until they were on the motorway, approaching Oxford, that he made reference to her meeting with Jon. 'Do you often do this?' he asked casually. 'Meet halfway for lunch?'

'No, not really.' She shook her head. 'But there are things we need to discuss. There wasn't time last weekend, what with the wedding and everything...' She trailed off, reluctant somehow to give any reasons for this meeting, unable to cope with what his reaction might be and at the same time grateful that he seemed to accept her silence by not asking any further questions, almost as if he, too, recognised the importance of the forthcoming meeting. As they left the motorway and entered the city, she told him where she had arranged to meet Jon. He stopped the car quite close to the pub and arranged a time when he would pick her up from the same place. As she moved to get out of the car he reached out, took her hand and squeezed it tightly.

'Omar—' she began, but he stopped her.

'No,' he said, 'not yet.'

As he drove away she suddenly felt very alone and a little bit lost, which was ridiculous really, knowing that in the space of the next few minutes she would be meeting Jon. Jon, whom she'd known for ever, Jon who was like...like a brother to her.

When she entered the pub and her eyes had grown accustomed to the dim light inside she saw that Jon was already there. Seated at a table in a secluded corner, he had a glass in front of him and was reading something on a folded newspaper that lay before him. He was casually dressed in jeans and a sweatshirt and as she approached Sandie felt a pang at what she was about to do, a pang which was suddenly intensified as he looked up, caught sight of her, smiled and stood up. What if her assumptions were correct and his intention was indeed to ask her to marry him? Could she really be that cruel, that callous to turn him down? Deep down she knew there was no question. If that was what was about to happen, she knew that was what she had to do.

'Sandie, hello.' He kissed her on the cheek. 'Let me get you a drink.'

'Hello, Jon.' She smiled and sat down. 'A spritzer would be nice.'

She watched him as he went to the bar. Knowing him as well as she did, she could see that he was nervous. Suddenly she, too, felt nervous and wiped the palms of her hands down the front of her trousers, wishing this meeting was over and she was heading back to Sussex with Omar.

When Jon returned with her drink, they chatted amiably enough about the weather, her journey—she carefully avoided saying she had come with Omar—and about their respective jobs. But inevitably they ran out of small talk and the moment arrived when each of them knew that no longer could they delay the true reason for this meeting.

After a lengthy silence they both began speaking at once and laughed nervously. Jon said, 'Go on. After you.'

'When I spoke to you on the phone, you said you needed to see me,' said Sandie at last.

'And you said the same thing,' he replied. 'So who's going to go first?'

Sandie took a deep breath. 'Do you mind if I do?' she said. Suddenly she felt it imperative that she let him know how she felt in the hope that it might prevent him from humiliating himself too much if it was indeed his intention to propose to her.

'Be my guest,' he said. He spoke warily but Sandie thought she detected a faint note of relief in his voice.

'Jon, I don't really know how to say this,' she began, 'but lately I have felt that our relationship has changed. I'm not sure that I can really explain this, but in a way I feel we are simply drifting…as if we aren't really going anywhere…'

'Sandie, I—'

'No. Please,' she said, interrupting him. 'Please, Jon, please, let me finish.'

'Go on,' he said helplessly.

'Well, I've thought long and hard about this and I tried to analyse how I felt about the situation…'

'And did you come to any conclusions?' He threw her a wary glance.

'Yes,' she replied, 'I did. I think…I think, Jon, it would be better if we changed the boundaries of our relationship.'

'In what way?' He frowned.

'Well, I couldn't imagine us ever being anything other than friends,' she said slowly. 'Let's face it, we've known each other for ever, but maybe the time has come to release each other from the bounds of the relationship as we've come to know it…'

'You mean no sex?' he said with a sudden grin.

'Well, yes, that of course…' She floundered a little, thrown slightly by this unexpected spark of humour.

'Sorry,' he said. 'Go on.'

'Well, that's it really.' She shrugged helplessly. 'I feel our affair, relationship, call it
what you like, has run its course. I'm sorry,
Jon, I don't want to hurt you, I really don't...'

'It's OK,' he said, then took a huge mouthful of his drink. 'I do understand, Sandie, believe me.'

She stared at him. 'Was that...what you
were going to say as well?' she began tentatively, some sixth sense telling her that this
might be so.

'Sort of,' he replied. Throwing her a tenta-
tive glance, he said, 'but it's a bit more than
that. I couldn't tell you last week when I came
down because I didn't think a wedding was the
appropriate time, and I didn't know how I was
going to tell you...but somehow you've just
made it easier for me.'

'I have?'

'Yes.' He inhaled deeply and began flexing
the fingers on his left hand. 'The truth is,
Sandie, I've met someone else...'

She stared at him in disbelief, suddenly unable to take in what he was saying. 'You've
met someone else,' she said stupidly at last.

'Yes,' he replied, 'yes, I have. She's a staff nurse at Chester and her name is Kirsty.' He paused as a man made his way past their table with a tray of drinks. 'I fought it for a long time, Sandie,' he went on at last, 'because of us, but I can't fight it any longer...and the truth is I don't want to fight it any longer.'

'When did it start?' she asked faintly.

'A few months ago,' he admitted.

She frowned. 'When I was in Manchester?'

'Yes, but, like I say, I fought it to start with...'

'Is that why you didn't stay over when you came down for the wedding?' she asked.

'Yes.' He nodded. 'I'm sorry, Sandie, really I am. I didn't mean for it to happen, I wasn't looking for it, but, well...I simply can't explain it. I only know it feels right when I'm with her. I don't expect you to understand.'

Sandie was silent for a long moment as the sounds and activities of the pub went on around them. She could hardly believe what Jon had just told her, that far from proposing to her he had come to tell her that he was in love with someone else. Surely she should be feeling hurt and betrayed—instead of which, the feeling that was slowly creeping over her was one of intense relief, relief that she wouldn't have to turn down any proposal from Jon and relief that there was now a distinct possibility that they would be able to remain friends.

'Actually, Jon,' she said at last, 'maybe I do understand...'

His eyes widened as he looked at her. 'Is there someone else for you, too?' he asked gently.

'Not exactly,' she replied, 'not in the same way as for you. But I have been attracted to someone and maybe it was that which made me question my feelings for you.'

'This someone else,' said Jon. 'It wouldn't by any chance be a certain registrar at Ellie's, would it?'

Sandie felt colour flood her cheeks. 'It might be,' she replied guardedly.

'I'm not surprised,' Jon replied with a grin. 'Don't think I didn't notice the way he was looking at you last Saturday.'

'That's as may be,' Sandie replied, almost primly, 'but things aren't that easy. He already has a girlfriend.'

'Ah,' said Jon, 'the flamboyant Amanda.'

'Yes,' Sandie agreed, 'plus the fact that I made things perfectly plain to Omar that because of you I simply wasn't interested in another relationship.'

'Well, if he's anything like Kirsty, he will have recognised the real thing when he saw it and be prepared to wait,' observed Jon shrewdly.

'I don't know how we are going to tell our families,' said Sandie after a moment.

'No,' Jon agreed, 'that could be tricky. They need to be told at the same time, I think.'

'Yes,' Sandie agreed, 'and we need to stress the fact that our decision is mutual. I suggest we ring them tonight and tell them.'

They both relaxed somewhat after that and ordered lunch, and when at last they parted, Jon to drive back to Chester and Sandie, with a little time on her hands before she was due to meet Omar, to do a little shopping, it was with a kiss and a hug, as the best of friends.

Sandie was waiting at the agreed meeting place when Omar drew up, and as she climbed into the car she leaned against the headrest with a deep sigh and briefly closed her eyes.

'Are you all right?' he asked, casting her a concerned sideways glance.

'Yes, I'm fine,' she replied.

They drove in silence for a time, giving Sandie an opportunity to collect her thoughts and reflect on her meeting with Jon. She had been amazed at what he had told her but in the end it had made her own mission very much easier. In her heart she wished Jon all the luck in the world and hoped fervently that he would find true happiness with his Kirsty. If only things could be as simple and as straightforward for herself. She allowed herself a surreptitious glance at Omar. His brow was lowered as he concentrated on the road ahead but her heart turned over at the sight of his profile and his strong hands on the steering-wheel.

'Did…did you see your grandparents?' she asked at last, breaking the silence between them.

'Yes, I did.' He nodded. 'They were surprised and delighted to see me. I was, in fact, their second visitor this week—the other was my cousin Ramani, Mitzi's son. He's in this country trying to raise awareness of the plight of some of our people in Somalia. He met my grandparents when I took them to Africa and he promised them he would visit them if he was ever in this country. He will be coming to see me in a few days' time.' He paused. 'How was your meeting with Jon?' he asked at last.

'It went very well,' Sandie replied. 'We both had a reason for wanting to see each other,' she added.

'Am I to be allowed to know what those reasons were?' asked Omar tentatively. While they had been talking he had left the motorway and was now driving more slowly on smaller country roads.

'I don't see why not.' Sandie gave a little shrug. 'I wanted to see Jon to tell him that I felt our relationship wasn't going anywhere, that in its present form it had run its course.'

Beside her she felt Omar's body tense. 'And how did he take that?' he asked at last.

'Better than I had feared,' Sandie replied. 'I was afraid that he might think I was wanting marriage to bring about the necessary change in the relationship.'

'And weren't you?' asked Omar quietly.

'It may have been what I wanted once,' she replied guardedly, 'but it isn't what I want now.'

'I see.' He paused again. 'So what about Jon? Why did he want this meeting?'

'He wanted to tell me that he has met someone else and has fallen deeply in love with her.'

With a smothered exclamation Omar swerved the car into a lay-by and switched off the engine. 'You're joking!' he said, half turning in his seat to face her, his expression one of astonishment.

'I can assure you I'm not,' she replied. 'He said he met her a few months ago but had fought his feelings because of our long-term relationship. But gradually he'd come to realise that he couldn't fight the feelings any longer.'

'So he knew all this when he came down for the wedding?' Omar still looked astounded.

'Yes,' Sandie said, 'but he said he felt a wedding was neither the time nor the place to end a relationship.'

'Well!' Omar shook his head. 'I said when he drove back to Chester that night that he must be mad to leave you. Now I know for sure that he is.'

'No, Omar.' Sandie shook her head. 'Not mad, just a man who had become very confused by the intensity of his feelings—something which...I...I can identify with,' she admitted at last.

Omar stared at her then as her meaning became clear he leaned forward and very gently touched her lips with his own.

At the touch of his lips the magic was back. Sandie drew back and gently touched his mouth with her fingers. 'You are forgetting something,' she said softly.

'Oh?' he replied, allowing his gaze to roam hungrily over her face—her eyes, her hair, her cheeks and finally once more on her lips. 'And what is that?'

'You still have Amanda,' she said softly.

Leaning forward, Omar again kissed her. Between kisses he said, 'I finished my relationship with Amanda three days ago.'

Sandie stared at him in astonishment. This was the last thing she had been expecting to hear. 'Well,' she said at last, 'this has indeed turned out to be a day of surprises.'

'So this leaves both you and me free,' said Omar, gently touching her face with the backs of his fingers.

'Yes...' she agreed slowly, 'it does. But, Omar, I need some time...'

'Of course you do,' he said softly. 'You need space to come to terms with all that has happened.'

'It's just that Jon and I have been together for a very long time and...' She trailed off with a helpless little gesture. Suddenly she felt over-whelmingly tired as the tension and the events of the day caught up with her.

'I intend to give you all the time you need,' he said softly. 'We will take this very slowly. I believe that what we have discovered is far too precious to rush in any way...so right now I'm going to take you home.'

'Oh, yes,' she replied, allowing her head to rest briefly on his shoulder. 'Yes, please.'

'So let me get this straight. You and Jon have split up and he has someone else?' Penny stared at Sandie in astonishment. It was a week later and the two of them were sharing lunch in the staff canteen.

'Yes,' Sandie said. When Penny seemed too stunned to continue she went on, 'It's been coming for some time. I knew our relationship had changed…'

'But you must be devastated,' said Penny, finding her voice at last. 'You and Jon have been together for…well, for a long time.'

'You were going to say for ever, weren't you?' said Sandie with a little smile.

'Well, what I meant was…'

'No, it's OK.' Sandie sighed. 'You're right and the truth was it simply wasn't going anywhere. I think we both realised it about the same time.'

'You mean you wanted to end it as well?' Penny's eyes narrowed.

Sandie nodded. 'I just woke up to the fact one day that I didn't want to marry Jon any longer—quite honestly, Penny, I realised I didn't love him in that way any more.'

'So was there a reason for all this?'

'Well, like I say, Jon has met someone else and I think he realised that this is the real thing and that what we had wasn't.'

'OK,' said Penny, 'it happens. But what about you? Have you met someone else and realised the same thing?'

'Actually, yes, I think I have.' Sandie felt warm colour flood her cheeks.

'Am I allowed to know the name of this charmer who seems to have succeeded where…?' Penny trailed off as suspicion suddenly seemed to flare in her eyes. 'Don't tell me it's Omar?' she demanded suddenly.

'Well, actually…'

'Oh, Sandie!' Penny couldn't hide her dismay.

'What's wrong with him, for heaven's sake?' demanded Sandie, suddenly stung into defending Omar.

'Nothing,' said Penny instantly. 'There's nothing wrong with Omar. He's a lovely man…but…'

'But what? It's just because he has a bit of a reputation, isn't it?'

'That's putting it mildly. He's broken plenty of hearts, Sandie, even in the short time he's been at Ellie's.'

'He can't help it if women find him irresistible,' declared Sandie hotly.

'And what about Amanda?' demanded Penny suddenly.

'He finished his relationship with Amanda nearly two weeks ago,' said Sandie, once more coming to Omar's defence.

'Really?' Penny looked surprised. 'I haven't heard anything about that,' she said slowly.

'Well, he did.'

'So have you been seeing one another?'

'Yes,' Sandie admitted, 'yes, we have. Nothing spectacular. I told him I wanted time to come to terms with things and he agreed so, you see, he isn't quite the ruthless womaniser you had him down for.'

'You haven't slept with him yet?'

'No, of course not,' Sandie replied indignantly. 'I told you, we are taking things very slowly. I cooked him supper one night, he took me out to dinner on another—and that's about it for the moment.'

'Well, I can see it's no earthly good warning you off any further but do take care, Sandie. I would hate him to use you, then hurt you by moving on to the next one.'

'I'll bear it in mind,' said Sandie, but there was a little smile playing around her mouth as she spoke.

'You're smitten, aren't you?' said Penny flatly.

'Do you know, Penny, I believe I am. I don't think I have ever felt this way before in my life. I have been with Jon for as long as I can remember and it was never like this. I feel so alive somehow with Omar—so full of anticipation.'

'Have you told your parents yet?'

'I told them that Jon and I have parted but I haven't told them about Omar yet,' Sandie replied.

'How did they take it—about you and Jon splitting up, I mean?'

'They were pretty upset,' Sandie admitted, 'especially my mum. She'd been busy planning a wedding—but she'll get over it. Jon's mother was the biggest problem—she threw an absolute fit, apparently.'

'Oh, well, like you say, they'll get over it in time.' Penny stood up and smoothed down her uniform. 'I'd better get back,' she said. 'We've got several admissions this afternoon.' She paused and looked at Sandie again. 'Have you met any of Omar's family?' she asked curiously at last.

'I met his cousin the night before last,' she replied. 'He's over from Somalia at the moment.'

'Is he like Omar?'

'In some ways,' Sandie said. 'He has that same regal bearing that Omar has and the same, almost old-fashioned charm, but you have to remember that Omar's mother was English whereas both Ramani's parents are Somali, and that Omar was raised and educated in this country by his grandparents.'

'I didn't know that,' said Penny slowly. 'What happened to Omar's parents?'

'They were killed in Africa when he was a boy,' Sandie replied quietly. 'His grandparents are still alive and live near Oxford. They think the world of Omar—' She broke off as her pager suddenly sounded and, jumping to her feet, she switched it off. 'I must go, too,' she said.

'See you later, Sandie,' said Penny as she made her way to the door. 'Oh, and, Sandie?'

She paused, one hand on the doorhandle. 'I do want you to be happy, you know.'

'Yes, Pen, I know you do,' Sandie replied.

'Just be careful—right? Don't rush into anything you may live to regret.'

'OK.' She smiled and picked up the telephone receiver to find out where she was needed next.

'Dr Rawlings to Special Care Baby Unit, please,' said the voice on the other end of the line.

'I'm on my way,' Sandie replied.

The moment Sandie set foot in the special care baby unit she knew that something was wrong. Both paediatricians, Matt Forrester and Suzanne Purcell, together with Omar and Louise, were in Louise's office. Sandie would have slipped unnoticed into the back of the room but for Omar, who gave her the secret smile they had adopted for whenever they met on the wards. It was only then that she realised that Pete Simmonds was also in the room and her heart sank.

'What is it?' she whispered to Omar as Pete sat down at the desk to sign some papers.

'Natasha has taken a turn for the worse,' Omar murmured back, just loud enough so that only Sandie could hear.

'Oh, no!' Sandie's face creased into a worried frown. 'Marcus Lichfield is away, isn't he?'

'He is.' Omar nodded. 'In Canada, to be precise. The duty cardiologist has decided that Natasha should be moved to London for immediate surgery.'

'But I thought she was too small,' protested Sandie, turning slightly so that she could see through the glass panel and across the corridor to the HDU where she caught a glimpse of Lizzie as she maintained her vigil at her baby daughter's side.

'It's her only chance,' Omar replied softly. Indicating for Sandie to open the door and go outside, he joined her in the corridor. 'If they don't operate she won't survive another day. If they do, there is a chance that the operation will be a success.'

'How are they going to transport her?' asked Sandie.

'Airlift her,' Omar replied. 'A helicopter is coming for her in about an hour. Matt wants you and me to supervise the handover. Apparently there will be a doctor and a nurse on board as escort and, of course, Lizzie and Pete will go with her.'

'In that case, I suggest we go and make the necessary preparations,' Sandie replied.

They found Lizzie in a surprisingly upbeat, optimistic frame of mind. 'At least something is to be done,' she said, looking up at them, 'instead of this dreadful watching and waiting for any little sign of deterioration. I only wish Mr Lichfield was here.' She turned her gaze back to her daughter whose tiny form was barely visible beneath the mass of tubes that were necessary for her very existence.

'She is going to one of the finest children's hospitals in the world,' said Sandie.

'And I understand from Dr Forrester that Charles Bannerman will perform the operation—he's one of the top cardiac surgeons in the country,' added Omar.

'I know,' said Lizzie, blinking back her tears. 'Everyone has been wonderful and one day Natasha herself will know just how hard everyone fought to save her life.'

The next hour was taken up in intense preparation as Natasha was prepared for her journey. Together with Louise, Sandie and Omar carried out the baby's observations of temperature, blood pressure and heart rate, entering them all into the records that would accompany her. Her medication was adjusted and checked and she was made dry and comfortable before being placed in a specially heated and prepared portable incubator. Lizzie and Pete, who had hardly left the hospital since their daughter's birth, sleeping at night in the parents' room alongside the unit, hurriedly collected their belongings which Pete stowed in the boot of their car. They had already agreed that Pete would drive to London while Lizzie accompanied Natasha in the helicopter.

They had barely finished when word came through that the helicopter was about to land in the field behind Ellie's. With Omar wheeling the incubator with its precious occupant and a mass of equipment through the maze of hospital corridors, Sandie walked alongside with Louise, who wanted to see her tiny charge safely aboard the helicopter, and Lizzie, who had just said a tearful goodbye to Pete who was anxious to be on his way to London.

They left the hospital through a rear door that was not used by the public and as they stepped outside into the warm autumn sunshine they could all see the silver helicopter as it came down to land on the grass. The door opened and, accompanied by the others, Omar wheeled the incubator forward.

A doctor and nurse were waiting to receive their tiny charge but both Omar and Sandie climbed aboard to make sure the new team was completely familiar with Natasha's condition and what would be required on the flight to London.

At last they were satisfied that all was well, and with a last little glance of farewell towards the baby who slept in some dark, secret world of her own and a word of encouragement to Lizzie, Sandie and Omar left the helicopter. By the time they returned to the hospital entrance Louise had gone back to her other charges on SCBU. With a sudden whirring of rotor blades the helicopter was airborne, turning in its ascent as it headed for London. They watched until it was no more than a tiny silver speck in the sky then Sandie swallowed and turned to Omar.

'Do you think she has a chance?' she asked.

'Yes, I do,' he replied, 'and Matt and the others must think so otherwise they wouldn't be putting her through all this.'

'Oh, I do hope you're right,' said Sandie with a sigh as Omar shut the doors and they began the long walk back to SCBU. 'Lizzie and Pete have been so brave over it all. I'm not sure I would be the same if that were my baby.'

'Do you want children, Sandie?' he asked softly.

'Oh, yes,' she replied passionately. 'Yes, I do. Not immediately, of course, but one day. One day I would love a family.'

'Me, too,' he replied. They walked in silence for a while then he said, 'Would you like to go to Angelo's tonight?'

'That sounds nice.' She threw him a quick smile.

'I'll book us a table,' he replied.

'I don't finish until late so I'll need to go straight there,' said Sandie.

'Eight o'clock?'

'Eight o'clock it is.' She was aware of a warm little glow somewhere in the pit of her stomach as she anticipated the evening ahead, for slowly, gradually she knew that she was falling deeply in love with the handsome registrar who walked beside her. Instinct told her that it was the same for him and that he was falling in love with her. She had listened to Penny's warnings but somehow it seemed as if her friend was talking about someone else entirely because as she got to know Omar even better, Sandie found herself doubting that he would ever simply use her then move on to his next conquest. That, quite simply, was not in keeping with the Omar she had come to know.

CHAPTER TEN

'DR SANDIE!' Maria Fabiano bustled forward to greet Sandie as she entered Angelo's Restaurant that evening after finishing her shift. 'Is lovely to see you! But we fully booked tonight—we have no tables.' She spread her hands apologetically.

Sandie glanced quickly around the restaurant but there was no sign yet of Omar. 'It's all right, Maria,' she said. 'I'm meeting someone—Dr Omar,' she added.

'Ah!' Maria eyed her speculatively for barely two seconds but the look spoke volumes. 'Yes, Dr Omar, he have table booked.' Turning, she led the way through the restaurant to a secluded little alcove, its walls covered with Latin script and scenes of ancient Rome. 'This your table,' she said, turning to Sandie. 'I get you a drink while you wait?'

'Yes, thank you, Maria—a mineral water would be nice.'

Moments later Maria was back with a tray bearing a glass of iced mineral water. 'Tell me, Maria.' Sandie looked up at the woman as she placed the glass on the table. 'How is Sophia?'

'I was just going to tell you.' Maria beamed. 'She much better.'

'Really? You mean the cream is working?'

'Well, she stop scratching,' said Maria, spreading her hands in an expressive shrug. 'But we also see to that other thing you talk about.'

Sandie frowned. 'The other thing?'

'Yes, you talk about stress. I know Sophia not been happy at school so I go down there and sort it out. She being bullied by other girls. They call her names, steal her books and hide her lunch, but it sorted now.'

'What did you do, Maria?' asked Sandie in awe.

'No matter what I do.' The Italian woman's dark eyes flashed. 'They not bother my daughter again.' She turned as if to walk away then she stopped and looked down at Sandie again. 'How your Jon?' she asked curiously.

'He's very well, thank you, Maria,' Sandie replied. She would have left it there but at that moment out of the corner of her eye she saw Omar come into the restaurant. As her heart missed a beat a sudden impulse prompted her to offer Maria an explanation, knowing that if she didn't she and Omar would come under fierce scrutiny and be the cause for much speculation. 'Jon and I have finished our relationship, Maria,' she said.

'Oh, Sandie!' The woman stared at her in concern.

'It's all right,' Sandie said quickly. 'It was mutual. Jon has a new lady in his life...' She paused, breaking off as by that time Omar had reached the alcove. Maria turned and caught sight of him.

'Ah, Dr Omar,' she said.

'Good evening, Maria,' he replied. His eyes on Sandie, he went on, 'Forgive me, Sandie, I was delayed.'

'It's all right.' She smiled, and her joy at seeing him must have been apparent. Maria looked from one to the other as realisation dawned. With a rich chuckle she took Omar's order for a drink then hurried back to the kitchen, no doubt to impart the news to her husband.

'A patient?' asked Sandie sympathetically as Omar sat down opposite her.

'No.' He shook his head. 'A call from Ramani, actually,' he said.

'Oh? Isn't he going home tomorrow?'

'Yes.' Omar appeared to hesitate then, as if reaching a decision, he said, 'I wasn't going to tell you this but the reason that Ramani came here in the first place—apart from trying to raise funds and create awareness of his work— was to try to persuade me to go out to Somalia and work in the new health clinic he has helped to set up.'

At his words Sandie felt her stomach turn over. As Maria brought his drink and two menus, she found herself wondering if she had found Omar only to lose him again almost as quickly. The thought in itself was almost intolerable.

'I told him no,' he said at last, as Maria moved away out of earshot. 'I said it was out of the question. Tonight he phoned again in one last attempt to make me change my mind.'

'But hasn't that always been your desire, what you've always dreamed of doing?' It had to be said in spite of her dread. 'Didn't you tell me once that one day you wanted to go to Africa and work, to help to ease some of the terrible suffering and poverty?'

'Yes,' he said, the dark eyes growing serious. 'Yes, Sandie, I did. But that was before you came into my life.' He paused and in the silence Sandie's heart was beating so loudly she feared he could hear it. 'I can't go now. I don't want to leave you,' he said simply. Reaching out, he covered her hand where it lay on the table with one of his own. At his words, spoken so simply but with so much passion, Sandie felt the breath catch in her throat. 'I think now,' he went on, 'we should talk of something else. I had a call from Matt,' he said, his tone lightening considerably, 'just before I left the hospital. He said Natasha had come through the operation.'

'That's wonderful!' Sandie stared at him.

'The next few days will, of course, be crucial,' he added, 'but the operation was successful and they have every reason to hope that she will survive.'

'Lizzie and Pete must be so relieved,' said Sandie. 'It must be one of the hardest things in the world when the life of your child is in the balance.'

They talked of other things while they enjoyed Angelo's mouth-watering pasta dishes—of places they had visited, books, films and music, their friends and, inevitably, their families.

'I want you to come to Woodstock with me and meet my grandparents,' said Omar as he refilled their glasses with the excellent red Italian wine Angelo had recommended.

'I should like that,' Sandie replied. 'Likewise, you must come to Norfolk with me and meet my family.'

'Do they know about me yet?' he asked, his gaze meeting hers across the table.

'Oh, yes,' she replied. 'I told my sister Vicky, who promptly told my mother, who rang me back at the first opportunity.'

'Was she upset about you and Jon?' asked Omar.

'Surprisingly, no,' Sandie replied thoughtfully. 'I rather gather that she was becoming concerned at how our relationship seemed to be dragging on and not really going anywhere.'

'My grandparents can't wait to meet you,' said Omar.

'What did Ramani say when you turned down his offer?' asked Sandie curiously.

'He…he was disappointed,' Omar replied, and Sandie got the impression that for her benefit his choice of word grossly played down his cousin's true reaction.

'He must have been pretty sure that you would want to join him in this project,' she said slowly.

'Well, yes,' Omar agreed, 'I suppose he was. We had spoken about it many times, you see…' He trailed off into a slightly uneasy silence.

'Tell me about it,' she said.

'I'm not sure there's much point,' he began, but she interrupted him.

'Please,' she said. 'I'd like to know.'

'OK.' He shrugged. 'Well, as you no doubt already know, for decades now much of Somalia has been torn apart by civil unrest, leaving the population grossly impoverished in terms of utilities and health care. Ramani was desperate to do something to improve conditions in the area where he was born, where his mother Mitzi still lives and where my own father was born. I was able to put him in touch with various aid organisations and charities in this country and help with fundraising. He has achieved a lot already and has now managed to set up this health-care centre to the west of Mogadishu.'

'And he hoped that you would go out there to run it—is that right?' asked Sandie quietly.

'Something like that, yes.' Omar nodded then looked away. 'But, like I told you, things have changed now. I have told Ramani that I have at last met someone who means the whole world to me—'

'When would all this have happened?' asked Sandie, interrupting him.

'What do you mean?' Omar frowned.

'Well, when would you have gone out there?'

'In three months' time,' he replied, 'but I told you—'

'No, Omar, listen.' Sandie held up her hand and he fell silent. 'Presumably,' she went on, 'this centre will want other medical staff, other doctors?'

'Well…yes,' he agreed warily.

'What if I were to say that I would go out there as well?' she said at last. Omar stared at her, apparently stunned into silence. 'I could, you know,' she went on rapidly. 'I don't know much about tropical medicine, though I'm sure there must be some sort of course I could do. But I do have my paediatric experience and I guess, well, children are children whatever part of the world they happen to be.'

For a moment, while she'd been speaking, hope and excitement had flared in Omar's dark eyes. As she stopped, reason seemed to take over again and he sighed.

'Sandie,' he said, 'I am honoured that you should consider doing this for me but there is no way I could even ask such a thing of you.'

'You aren't asking it of me,' she said. 'I'm volunteering. And if you remember, when I first met you and we spoke of working in underprivileged areas I said it was something I had already considered doing. Africa has always fascinated me,' she went on when the doubt persisted in his eyes. 'And from your descriptions of the place, it sounds wonderful.'

'It is wonderful,' he agreed slowly. 'But there is another side, Sandie,' he went on, his voice taking on an urgent note now as if it was somehow imperative he make his point. 'A side I may not have dwelt on but which nevertheless is very real. A side of poverty and deprivation, of famine, pestilence and disease. AIDS is a desperate problem, as is child mortality, TB has increased in the last few years…'

'All the more reason for trained doctors.'

'It would be tough, Sandie, very tough.'

'You don't think I'm up to it, is that what you're saying?' she demanded. 'That because I'm a woman—'

'No,' he interrupted her, shaking his head, 'that is not what I'm saying at all. What I am saying is that I don't want to put you through that. You have a good job here at Ellie's, your family is here, your friends…'

'And all that would presumably still be here if I found I couldn't cope with the conditions you describe,' she said. 'But if I don't try, don't give it a go, I will never know. And if I don't go and you remain here as well, they will have lost the services of not one but two doctors. From what you have told me, it doesn't sound as if that is the sort of loss Ramani's health centre could withstand.'

'Maybe not.' Omar spread his hands. 'But, Sandie, I couldn't ask you to give up everything for me.'

'You aren't asking me, I'm offering,' said Sandie flatly. 'That's a different thing altogether. Besides, you were prepared to give everything up for me so there's no earthly reason why I shouldn't do the same—unless, of course...'

'Unless what?' Omar's eyes narrowed slightly as he looked at her.

'Unless you wouldn't want me to go out there with you,' she said quietly, wondering if perhaps she had simply assumed too much.

'Sandie.' Omar set down his knife and fork and stared at her. 'There is nothing on this earth that I would like better, believe me—to fulfil the dream of a lifetime with the woman I love by my side...'

'I can feel a ''but'' coming,' said Sandie warily.

'I was going to say that I still feel it is too much to expect of you,' he went on.

She stared thoughtfully at him for a long moment through half-closed eyelids then, coming to a decision, she said, 'Supposing I were to say I would do it for a year?'

'A year?' He frowned.

'Yes,' she replied. 'At the end of that time we could reassess the situation. If I like the work, the country, the climate, we stay on. If not, we come back to England. What do you say?'

'I say it sounds incredible,' he said at last.

'But you are willing to give it a try?' she persisted.

'Well, yes,' he said slowly at last. 'How could I refuse such an offer? That is, of course, if you are absolutely sure it is what you want.'

'Absolutely,' she said, 'so I suggest you phone Ramani as soon as we get back to Pitt's Place.'

Omar came to her apartment on their return and made his phone call to Ramani from there. Sandie could not help but overhear him as she made coffee, and as she heard the excitement and enthusiasm in his voice as he told his cousin what they had decided, her heart was suffused with love for him.

'What time is your flight tomorrow?' she heard him say. 'Good, I'll come over to see you in the morning and we can discuss some of the details before you go.'

'He is overjoyed,' he said a few moments later when he came into the kitchen. He slipped his arms around her as she stood waiting for the kettle to boil. 'He sends you his greetings and his heartfelt thanks for the huge sacrifice you are prepared to make for his...for our people.'

'I don't feel like it's a sacrifice,' she said, leaning back in his arms. 'I feel like it's the start of an adventure.'

'You can have no idea of the gratitude that will be felt by those people you are going to help,' he said. 'And for you it will be taking a step into the unknown.'

'If you are by my side, it won't feel like that,' she said.

'And I will be,' he promised. 'Every step of the way,' he murmured as, lowering his head, he kissed the hollow between her neck and shoulder. A shaft of pure pleasure coursed through her veins and she turned her head to allow him to continue this particular delight.

'Sandie…' His voice was suddenly husky, thick with desire, and with a little moan she twisted in his arms until she was facing him. Raising his arms, he took her face between his hands, tangling her hair in his fingers as, with his thumbs beneath her jaw, he tilted her face towards his. If in the past there had been any hesitation between them, now there was none as, with all barriers removed, his mouth claimed hers in a kiss so deep and full of longing that it removed any shred of doubt that might still have lingered. And when after a long time they eventually drew slightly apart it was only for Omar to bring her back, crushing her in his arms as once again his mouth claimed hers.

From there it was but a simple step to her bedroom. Where until that moment Sandie may have felt she needed more time to get used to this exciting new relationship, now all such reserve was swept away as Omar sat on the end of her bed and she stood before him between his knees while he undid the row of tiny buttons on the flimsy top she was wearing before sliding it off her shoulders and letting it fall to the floor. He unfastened the buckle on the belt of her skirt and as she felt it slip into a pool around her ankles she sank to her knees. Reaching out with hands that trembled with excitement and anticipation, she undid the buttons on his shirt and unbuckled his belt while he slipped his arms around her and unfastened the wispy piece of lace that was her bra.

His breath caught in his throat when he caught sight of her body and, taking her hands, he stood up, drawing her to her feet as well before leading her round to the side of the bed. As Sandie lay on the bed and waited for him to come to her, she watched him in the glow from the bedside lamp as he sat on the side of the bed. His body gleamed like polished amber, the crisp black hair, curled tightly along his neck and the muscles rippled across his naked back. Desire surged through her, crying out for release.

When at last he stretched out above her he took her into his arms and with lips and tongue and fingertips he took her to a place she'd never known, a place of such heightened desire she doubted she would ever recover from the

experience. And with a skill that left her helpless with delight he made sure that they soared
together, reaching the very pinnacle of their
passion simultaneously.

Even the descent from that high place was
exquisite as, amidst further waves of pleasure,
she gently tumbled back to earth. If for one
moment she'd imagined it to be over, she was
very much mistaken, for barely had she had
time to recover when he was reaching for her
again…and again.

With each time it was as if he found new
ways to please her, new delights to show her,
until in the end, utterly satiated and fulfilled,
she was begging him to stop while he, laugh-
ing at her protestations, told her he'd only just
begun.

The first pale fingers of dawn were filtering
through the curtains before finally they slept,
and when eventually Sandie woke up and remembered, she turned to look at the man who
slept at her side, one arm flung protectively
across her body, black lashes sweeping amber
cheeks. She knew without a shadow of doubt
that she had found her mate.

*   *   *

They agreed not to talk about their plans at Ellie's until official word came from Ramani on his return to Somalia. Neither did they speak to anyone else of their love for each other. The latter of these proved to be more difficult for Sandie for, while there was a part of her that wanted privacy to accept what was happening to her as she came to terms with the fact that she had fallen head over heels in love with Omar, there was another part which longed to tell everyone.

She couldn't remember a time in her life when she had been so happy—days spent at the work she loved, long nights in the arms of a lover both tender and exciting and the prospect of a future filled with adventure and tremendous fulfilment—so the blow, when it came, somehow had even more impact than it once might have done.

It was a day like any other with no hint of what was to come. The doctors and consultants had carried out their rounds of SCBU and the children's ward, where Sandie had stayed behind to talk to the physiotherapist who had arrived to see Sam.

'He's doing well,' said Sandie, smiling at Sam who grinned back at her. The boy had suffered quite a setback when he had learnt of Lewis's death but slowly he had recovered and was now well on the road to full mobility again.

'Yes,' the physiotherapist agreed, 'he is.'

'Does that mean I don't need to do my exercises today?' asked Sam hopefully.

'It most certainly does not,' the woman replied, 'and the sooner we get started, the sooner we finish. So come along, young man, we'll start by taking deep breaths.'

Sam pulled a face and with a smile Sandie moved away to the nurses' station where Penny was talking to nursery nurse Kimberley Graham. As Sandie approached the desk Emma suddenly appeared through the main doors of the ward, and from her expression it was obvious she was bursting to say something.

As she reached the desk she burst out, 'You'll never guess what I've just heard in the canteen.' She glanced over her shoulder as if to make sure that no one was listening who shouldn't be, then, leaning towards the others, she said— 'Amanda Cromer is pregnant!'

It took a moment for the full implication of what Emma had said to register in Sandie's brain, and it was Kimberley who reacted first. 'Well, that will curtail her activities a bit, won't it?' she said with a chuckle. 'Who's the father?'

'Well, it must be Omar, mustn't it?' Emma replied flippantly. 'He's the one she's been going with recently.'

For the space of one terrible moment the world seem to stand still as Sandie stared at Emma. Vaguely she was aware of the concerned glance Penny cast in her direction then, as the world started turning again, with a mumbled apology she turned away.

'Do you think she'll keep it?' she heard Kimberley say as she stumbled away from the desk.

'That's Amanda's business, not ours,' Penny replied. 'And I would say that's quite enough gossip for one day so can we, please, get back to work?'

Somehow she got through the rest of the day, in the event not seeing Omar again, knowing that first he was taking a clinic, then attending a consultants' meeting.

As the full impact of what Emma had revealed slowly sank in, Sandie knew that what had happened could change things for ever for herself and Omar. When he learnt of Amanda's pregnancy, if he didn't already know, being the honourable man that he was, he would feel obligated or might even want to take his full share of responsibility for the coming child. That Amanda was pregnant in the first place amazed Sandie because it somehow implied a lack of responsibility, even casualness on Omar's part, and certainly where she had been concerned he had been anything but casual, assuming full responsibility in their relationship. But it sounded as if it was too late for recriminations of that sort, just as it also sounded as if, by telling people, Amanda had already decided to proceed with the pregnancy.

How would this affect Omar in the future? Would he still be as keen to go ahead with their plans for Somalia or would he want to be a hands-on father who took an interest in his baby's welfare from the very beginning? And what of her? she asked herself wildly. How would she feel when Omar wanted to spend time with his child and inevitably with Amanda? Would she be able to cope with that on a day-to-day basis, with all three of them presumably still working in the same hospital?

Maybe she should end their relationship here and now—her heart twisted painfully at the very thought—release Omar from any obligation to her. Why, perhaps he would now even consider marrying Amanda so that the child she carried would bear his name. Maybe he was even now planning to finish with *her* so that he could be with Amanda.

Somehow she drove home to Pitt's Place, relieved to find that Omar wasn't yet home, knowing that, while these issues had to be addressed, she needed a little more time to think what her course of action should be. It would do no earthly good attacking Omar with every reproach she could think of, accusing him of irresponsibility and of toying with people's emotions and affections. That approach, she knew, would get her nowhere. No, she told herself firmly, this whole matter had to be addressed with calmness and dignity and resolved with the least possible turmoil for everyone concerned.

But by the time she heard the sound of Omar's car on the loose gravel of the drive she had worked herself up into a state of near panic, and the moment he set foot inside her apartment, instead of holding back and broaching the subject calmly as she had planned, to her eternal shame, she let fly.

'I'm surprised you bothered to come back here,' she snapped, rounding on him before he'd even had the chance to take his jacket off.

'I'm sorry?' He turned and stared at her.

'Unless, of course, you've simply come to pack,' she added bitterly.

'Sandie…?' There was bewilderment in his dark eyes now, a look that tore at her heart, but a look that no doubt he used with regularity, a look that ensured he would get his own way. 'Why would I want to pack?'

'Well, I imagine you will be moving out now.' Was that really her voice, so shrill, almost an octave higher than usual? Whatever was she doing? This was not at all what she had planned—but somehow she couldn't help herself. The pain of possibly losing Omar just when she had found such happiness with him was driving out every semblance of reason as a sort of madness took hold of her.

'Why would I want to move out?' He frowned.

'I can't imagine you would want to be with me—not now,' she went on bitterly. 'On the other hand, maybe you intend moving her into your apartment. Well, if that's the case I can assure you I shall be moving out. I certainly don't intend staying around to—'

'Sandie, please.' He made a move towards her. 'I have no idea what you are talking about. Move who in?'

She backed away, putting the sofa between them, believing she would be unable to bear it if he touched her, afraid her resolve would crumble. 'Amanda, of course.' She almost spat the words out in her pain and fury. 'Who did you think I meant?'

'But why would I want to move Amanda in here?' Omar's bewilderment was total now.

'Omar, please, stop playing games,' she said. 'You may have thought you could hide the truth from me up until now, but even you must have realised that I would find out sooner or later—it's not exactly something that can be hidden.'

'Sandie, I told you, my relationship with Amanda, such as it was, is over. I made that quite plain to her and I thought I had to you as well. I can't imagine why you should think any differently.'

'I didn't,' she said bitterly, 'not until I heard the truth. And while you may have successfully dismissed Amanda from your life, you may not find it so easy to dismiss a child. A child is for ever, Omar, not something that is created on a whim, something that will go away when irresponsible parents have tired of it.'

While she had been speaking Omar had grown very still, but his gaze never flinched or faltered and she had no idea what his thoughts might have been at that moment.

And then at last he spoke. 'Are you telling me that Amanda is having a child?' he asked quietly.

It was Sandie's turn to stare at him in amazement. 'You mean you didn't know?' she said at last. Surely Amanda wouldn't have told others before telling Omar himself.

'No,' he said, 'I didn't.' He turned his head slightly, staring at the floor. Looking up, he said, 'Well I'm glad, pleased for her.'

'You're *glad*?' Sandie spluttered. She hadn't been sure what his reaction would be but she certainly hadn't predicted this. 'How can you be glad?' Her voice was low now, barely more than a whisper.

'It was what she wanted,' he replied.

'What she wanted…?' Speechless and fighting a rising wave of anger, Sandie clutched at the top of the sofa, her fingers digging into the fabric.

'Yes,' he said. 'A baby might just put her life back on track again.'

'You mean it was deliberate—that it was planned?'

'Yes. It was what she wanted all along. I thought she might have told me about it, though.'

Hardly able to believe what she was hearing Sandie stared at him then at last from somewhere she found her voice again. 'How *could* you?' she said. 'How could you, Omar, how could you do that and then go on and start planning a life with me?'

As she spoke, her voice choking with emotion, Omar stared at her. Then the first glimmer of enlightenment entered his eyes. 'Sandie,' he said, 'you don't think…?'

'Please, don't.' She raised her hand. 'I don't want to hear any lies or excuses. I think it best that we should just part now…'

'Sandie, will you, please, listen to me?' Suddenly his voice was authoritative, forcing her to listen, and when he was sure he had her full attention he said, 'The baby isn't mine.'

She stared at him. 'Isn't yours?' she said in bewilderment.

'No,' he said, 'of course it isn't! Did you think that…?' He ran one hand over his head, the gesture one of tortured exasperation.

'Of course I did.' She spread her hands. 'What was I to think? You and she were in a relationship until very recently—there was gossip at work about Amanda being pregnant and it is being assumed that you must be the father.'

'And that is what you think?' His eyes darkened and for a moment she saw pain there, raw pain that she should have believed this of him.

'I didn't know what to think,' she protested helplessly. 'You and she were together, Omar, even before we met…'

'Yes,' he agreed, 'we were, but it isn't my baby, Sandie.'

'Isn't your baby…?' She frowned.

'You are wondering how I can be so sure, aren't you?' he said quietly, and there was a trace of accusation in his voice now.

'Well, Omar, you have to admit, it looks that way.'

'I know it isn't my baby because Amanda and I never slept together,' he said simply.

There was silence in the room, broken only by the faint sound of a clock as it chimed the hour in another part of the house.

'I never slept with Amanda,' said Omar at last, 'because I never loved her, and because I knew she didn't love me. When I sleep with a woman it has to be a shared expression of love and a sense of commitment, otherwise there is no point. I've been out with many women, Sandie, but that doesn't necessarily mean I sleep with them.'

'Oh, Omar…' Sandie whispered. A slow sense of devastation and guilt began to sweep over her that she could have doubted him in this way.

'Amanda was still in love with her husband,' he went on at last. 'She didn't recognise it at first but after I'd taken her out a few times she unburdened herself to me and gradually she came to acknowledge that fact. He had returned to her briefly for a couple of weeks before we started going out—I would lay odds that that was when this baby was conceived. On the night I told her we wouldn't be seeing each other again I persuaded her to contact her husband and she has told me since that she had done so and was hopeful of reconciliation. If people are assuming her baby is mine, Amanda needs to let them know otherwise.'

There was another lengthy silence in the room then slowly Sandie raised her eyes to meet his. 'I am so sorry,' she whispered, 'so very, very sorry. Can you ever forgive me?'

'I'm not sure about that,' he replied solemnly.

'Omar.' She swallowed. 'I should have trusted you. Please, I beg of you, please, forgive me.'

'It may be that I shall need much more persuasion.' He spoke in the same almost sombre tones but a gleam of wickedness had entered his eyes. 'After all, true remorse needs to come before forgiveness, and that is followed by penance, and only then can real reconciliation be enjoyed.'

'Omar…I…' Sandie stared at him in bewilderment but before she knew what was happening he covered the space between them and lifted her effortlessly up in his arms.

'And there's only one place where all this can happen,' he said. Crossing the room with her still in his arms, he pushed open the bedroom door, stepped inside then purposefully kicked the door shut behind them.

Three days later Omar had word from Ramani, following his return to Somalia. He came to find Sandie in the children's ward. 'Can you get away for a few minutes?' he asked softly.

'Penny, I need a few minutes' space,' she said.

'OK.' Penny looked from Sandie to Omar then back to Sandie again.

'We'll only be outside in the grounds if you should need us,' said Omar.

Together they made their way out of the building and walked across the soft mossy grass to their seat near the macrocarpas.

'You've heard from Ramani, haven't you?' she said as he sat down and touched the space beside him, inviting her to join him.

'Yes,' he said, 'I have.'

'And...?'

'The rest of the team are as delighted and excited as Ramani that I'm going to join them and that you also are coming.'

'That's wonderful,' she said. When he made no further comment she turned her head to look at him. 'Isn't it?' When he still didn't speak, she said, 'Omar?'

'Yes,' he replied at last, 'of course it is.'

'But...you seem troubled about something. What is it?'

He took a deep breath. 'This wasn't how I had planned this,' he said at last, 'but there's a bit of a question about status and accommodation...'

'What do you mean?' She frowned.

'Well, the accommodation they had prepared for me is a bungalow alongside the health centre…'

'Sounds lovely.'

'Don't get too excited. It will be pretty basic.'

'Even so…'

'The problem would be if we lived there together—you see, the group that has set up the health centre is part of a mission and they are very strict about things like that.'

'I see,' said Sandie slowly, 'but I'm still not certain what the problem is.'

'We would need to be married, Sandie, before we took up the position.'

'And that's a problem?' she said, reaching out her hand and gently running one finger down the side of his face.

He turned to look at her. 'You mean…?' he said, hope leaping in his dark eyes.

'Of course,' she replied. 'Did you doubt that I would?'

'I thought it might be too soon for you—that you would need more time.'

'Why should I need more time?' she said softly. 'I love you, Dr Nahum, with all my heart, and I know you love me. We have an exciting new life ahead of us—to start that life as man and wife is the best possible way.'

Taking her hand, he gently kissed her fingers one by one, then kissed the palm before closing her fingers firmly over the kiss. 'Dr Rawlings,' he said, his voice husky with emotion, 'do you know that you've just made me the happiest man on earth?'

'I shall need proof of that later,' she replied with a little sigh, 'but in the meantime I guess we had both better get back to work. And if the look on Penny's face was anything to go by when we came out, I would say we are going to have to do some explaining.'

'You're right,' he said as with a chuckle he stood up and drew her to her feet. 'It's time we told everyone anyway, and I think Penny just might be a very good place to start.'

MEDICAL ROMANCE™

Large Print

Titles for the next six months…

February

BUSHFIRE BRIDE	Marion Lennox
THE PREGNANT MIDWIFE	Fiona McArthur
RAPID RESPONSE	Jennifer Taylor
DOCTORS IN PARADISE	Meredith Webber

March

THE BABY FROM NOWHERE	Caroline Anderson
THE PREGNANT REGISTRAR	Carol Marinelli
THE SURGEON'S MARRIAGE DEMAND	Maggie Kingsley
EMERGENCY MARRIAGE	Olivia Gates

April

DOCTOR AND PROTECTOR	Meredith Webber
DIAGNOSIS: AMNESIA	Lucy Clark
THE REGISTRAR'S CONVENIENT WIFE	Kate Hardy
THE SURGEON'S FAMILY WISH	Abigail Gordon

MILLS & BOON®

Live the emotion

0105 LP 2P P1 Medical

MEDICAL ROMANCE™

Large Print

May

THE POLICE DOCTOR'S SECRET	Marion Lennox
THE RECOVERY ASSIGNMENT	Alison Roberts
ONE NIGHT IN EMERGENCY	Carol Marinelli
CARING FOR HIS BABIES	Lilian Darcy

June

ASSIGNMENT: CHRISTMAS	Caroline Anderson
THE POLICE DOCTOR'S DISCOVERY	Laura MacDonald
THE MIDWIFE'S NEW YEAR WISH	Jennifer Taylor
A DOCTOR TO COME HOME TO	Gill Sanderson

July

THE FIREFIGHTER'S BABY	Alison Roberts
UNDERCOVER DOCTOR	Lucy Clark
AIRBORNE EMERGENCY	Olivia Gates
OUTBACK DOCTOR IN DANGER	Emily Forbes

MILLS & BOON®

Live the emotion

0105 LP 2P P2 Medical